Death

at the

Water's Edge

Miriam Winthrop

CaliPress

Death at the Water's Edge is a work of fiction. Names, characters, and places, and locations are the product of the author's imagination or are used fictitiously. Any resemblance to actual events, locales, or persons, living or dead, is entirely coincidental.

Death at the Water's Edge is grounded in careful research. However, in support of the storyline, certain details have been changed.

The people of the Azores have been thoughtful about preserving their heritage. This series does not intend to imply otherwise, only to offer another way in which that gift could be managed.

Cover art photo credit: Myrabella / Wikimedia
Commons, via Wikimedia Commons CC-BY-SA-3.0
All other art is the property of Miriam Winthrop.

Published in the United States by CaliPress©.
CaliPress@comcast.net

ISBN 978-0692504680

1 Literary Fiction Themes/Friendship
2 Literary Fiction/Travel
3 Mystery Characters/Amateur Sleuth
4 Mystery Settings/Islands

To the memory of

Perrin Blythe Reid-Boelman

Where a beautiful soul has been, beautiful memories remain.

Death at the Water's Edge

1

Anton Cardosa felt the fate of his culture resting heavily on his shoulders, and the man lying on Farewell Beach threatened to make his burden even greater.

Golden light from a rising sun burnished a swath of the water surrounding the island and made long shadows of the five men standing by the shore. What was left of the Santa Maria police force, two full-time officers and two part-time volunteers, waited behind Anton. He was a large man, a foot taller and at least seventy pounds heavier than the others, so to the person watching the silhouetted figures from the hilltop, the group looked like an adult leading four children.

Taking great care not to trip over long ropes of seaweed left behind by the tide, Anton stepped back, walked a few feet away, and turned to face the small knot of men. Everyone followed him, but they avoided making eye contact, silently staring into the midrange or examining the sand at their feet.

Felipe Madruga, the oldest of the four finally spoke. "What would you like us to do, sir?"

Sir? Anton was at a loss. He wasn't familiar with situations such as this one. He had no background, no training, no interest in them whatsoever. He wasn't a police officer or a local official of any sort; he was a conservationist. But the letter bearing the presidential seal, the one he kept in a plastic sleeve on his desk, the one he hoped would lead to the preservation of his heritage, made the men think otherwise.

Only seven weeks earlier, Presidente Moniz had designated Anton as a Minister Plenipotentiary, recognized as speaking for him when he could not be reached. Such a role may have been made obsolete by technology in the twenty-first century, but the Presidente had a long history in the diplomatic corps, and he loved the pomp and circumstance of a bygone era. He had delighted in using his Mont Blanc fountain pen to put an oversize signature below the direction to offer Anton Luis Cabral Cardosa "… the full cooperation and deference of all, individually and collectively, in the defense and promotion of the culture of the Autonomous Region of the Azores."

Anton had pretended to listen seriously to the long monolog that followed, but actually he had been rejoicing with his inner boy. He had remembered nothing other than *I will give you a one-year trial.* Standing on the beach that morning, other words came back to him. *You will have one chance. If you fail, I will do nothing to save your position … or your cause.*

Long before ever being summoned to the beach, Anton had considered what he would do if he saw a dead body. When he read about someone who had come across the remains of a hiker at the bottom of one of the high cliffs that rimmed the island or when he watched the British crime shows that his wife, Catarina, liked so much, he decided he wouldn't have the bravery—if that's what it was—to look at a corpse. He was certain he would look away, walk away, call for one of those incomprehensible sorts who could even touch the dead. But that wasn't what happened. He hadn't been able to stop looking.

There was no doubt; the body lying on the beach was not someone in deep sleep or feigning death. The skin was unnaturally stiff and gray, and Anton knew it would feel cold and hard to the touch, like a stone statue in a museum. The eyes, fringed with lashes misted by the fog that had just rolled out to sea, were enormous discs of cloudy brown set in bluish whites, looking vacantly at the sky. Most of the hair looked auburn but where it had dried at the surface, he could see it was a bright copper, and the early morning sun shone through the wisps to give the head a glowing halo. What he saw at the top of the skull was the reason he had been called, a shallow depression that matched the bloodied rock Felipe had shown him before he had even turned off his car engine.

There was no dignity in this body, none of the little adjustments that people make as they present themselves to the world, no forced smile, no widening of the eyes, no smoothing of the hair. The seagull feather tucked behind the left ear like a quill pen actually made it look slightly ridiculous. The shirt had ridden up to expose a solid belly overhanging pants with a zipper half down. For several moments, Anton watched as reddish hairs on the white mound glinted in the morning light. Perhaps this is why people look away from the dead, he thought. Seeing the dead is like catching someone in an embarrassing situation, exposed and unable to mask weaknesses.

Anton tried to make himself respond to Felipe's question. *What did he want the men to do?* All he was sure of was that he had to decide quickly. When the call about the body came in, he was already late to pick up the woman who was crucial to his proposal. He worried that she was already waiting at the marina, perhaps past wondering where he was, perhaps ready to leave, taking the key to success with her. Normally, he wouldn't have been concerned over the delay of an hour or so. As in much of Europe, time in the Azores was flexible, an approximation of when friends would meet or how long a get-together would last. But he knew how impatient Americans were.

Anton realized Felipe had cleared his throat; he had heard it through the thrumming in his ears. Catarina said that when he heard his heartbeat, it meant his blood pressure was too high and he had to stop what he was doing, but he also knew no one would make a move without him. "Does anyone know who the ...." Was this simply a body? A victim? A person? "Does anyone know who the man ...," he hesitated again, then decided that the man still existed in enough of a form to use the present tense, "... is?"

They looked at each other, surprised. Felipe spoke up again. "Yes, sir. We all know. This is Frank, from Water's Edge." Santa Maria was a small island with a population of less than 15,000, so virtually everyone knew everyone else to one degree or another—everyone but newcomers and, after a twenty-five-year absence, Anton was just that.

All at once everyone was talking.

"It's Frank, Isabella's husband."

"Water's Edge. You know, by the caves."

"Everyone knows Frank Dekker."

"Should we get Padre Henriques?"

"Should we tell Isabella?"

"Poor Paolo."

"Should we move him before the tide comes in?"

"Where should we take him?"

Every time someone spoke, it was another delay. Anton was growing anxious. He wanted to pass this problem on to someone else quickly and get to the marina. At the same time, he knew he had to manage the unexpected turn of events in a way that would not compromise his plans for the next two weeks. He looked at Felipe and said in the most authoritative voice he could muster, "Go find Dr. Leal and bring him here. Tell him to examine ...," he almost said *it*, "... Frank." Emanuel Leal was the only doctor he knew of on the island, and he was semi-retired. He knew Maria Rosa Goulart, his neighbor, had been certified as a nurse and took care of many of the medical needs of residents and tourists, but she was young and emotional and loved to gossip. Not the best choice when his greatest concern was limiting news of what might have been the first murder on Santa Maria in living memory.

"Then take him to the basement of the police station." It was only a small stone building off the central square in the main city of Velo do Porto, but he knew it had a basement; that was where he had picked up his family's belongings when they arrived four weeks earlier.

He pointed at each one of them in turn as he slowly said, "You are not to let anyone know about this until I tell you to. Do you understand?" No one gave any indication that his words had made an impact. They just stood there looking stunned. *Merda*, thought Anton, I've gone too far. It's all falling apart—and before I had the chance to start. He took a gamble, hoping the four men believed that in the absence of the police chief, he had far more power than he actually did. "Your jobs depend on this!" The bark was uncharacteristic; Anton was a gentle man, with a normally calm, almost soothing voice.

Finally, they nodded over and over again.

"And take pictures," Anton commanded. "Lots of pictures." It's what the detectives in Catarina's favorite television shows always said. It was also the only other thing he could think of.

One of the policemen nervously stepped forward holding out a hand. Hanging from a gold chain looped around his index finger was a crucifix. "Um ... sir ...."

Anton felt sorry for the young man, one of the volunteers, but he forced himself to keep a stern expression. "Yes?"

"I found this." He extended his arm, his body language saying *Take it. I don't want to hold it.*

Anton took the crucifix and studied it. The patina on the wood cross told him it was quite old. The body of Jesus was beautifully rendered in painted porcelain. Hollowed eyes turned to heaven in both anguish and rapture, and the mouth seemed to be on the verge of asking a question. A chip marred the top of the head, exposing a snowy interior.

"It was over there," the young man said, pointing to a large boulder a few inches below the high tide mark.

The rock immediately brought to Anton's mind the image of a prehistoric sacrificial altar. He slowly walked in that direction, more to buy time than because he expected to find anything. It was pillow lava, created when magma forced its way to the surface and was quickly cooled by ocean water. The surface was smooth, almost glassy, and he could make out what looked like letters carved into the top.

MVI

A flash of white caught his eye. It was a fragment of the crucifix, smooth brown on the reverse side and so small surely it would have been washed away by the night's tide. He turned to ask someone to take a picture of the inscription, and he felt a tightening in his chest. The entire scene had been trampled by the four men, five if he included himself, and the crucifix he held in his hand had probably been passed around. He would never know if important evidence had been wiped away.

Not for the first time since he had been appointed by the Presidente, Anton felt inadequate. He hadn't handled this crisis well and if he couldn't do that, what hope was there for his proposal?

He allowed himself a moment to look up at the cluster of small stone buildings on one of the hills overlooking the beach. Catarina was there. She might be watching right now, knowing something was wrong but not knowing exactly what. Of all places, why had this happened in full view of Casa do Mar? If there was any trace of trouble in two weeks, his plans would be doomed. Feeling nauseous, he started back to his car and, without speaking a word, he waved his goodbyes to everyone with his back turned.

He folded his large frame into the Volvo wagon and sank into the well-worn seat. He inhaled deeply, exhaled slowly, and slammed the door shut. Then, perhaps for the first time in the car's ten-year history, he locked the doors.

Anton studied himself in the rearview mirror. His face looked as it always did: cheery. It had been both his blessing and his curse since childhood; bright brown eyes set below a lifted brow, rounded cheeks, and a perpetually upturned mouth gave the impression that he was a carefree sort. Most of the time, that only emphasized the disposition he was known for, appealing to friends and allies, attracting merriment and good times. Occasionally, it could give others the feeling that he was unfamiliar with worries of any sort, maybe not even up to dealing with something serious.

Buffered by the hush inside the locked car, the questions he wanted to ask—should have asked—came to him. Frank was a common nickname of those Franciscos who had emigrated to America and Canada, but it wasn't often heard locally. Was he a visitor or a summer resident? That would make everything worse. But if he was, why did the four men standing on the beach know his wife's name and that he was from Water's Edge? And what was Water's Edge? A house? A business? One of the coves where men got together to fish? The name tickled some dim corner of his mind but when he tried to bring it to light, the memory vanished.

He wanted to return to the beach, but he checked the clock on the dashboard and decided against it. The American woman waiting at the marina was of greater importance, he told himself. She was vital to his plan, and his plan was vital to his people. Anton started the car and sped away.

As he turned toward the Vila do Porto harbor, Anton remembered a day twenty-eight years before, when he caught sight of a red-haired girl climbing into a rowboat at the marina, and he thought about how that moment had changed the course of his life. Without that one glimpse, the body now being examined by Dr. Leal would not have mattered. Without that, his heart would not be thumping with hope about how the American woman could help him—or with fear about what would happen if his plans failed.

One word ricocheted in Lori Moore's mind: different. Everything was different: where she lived, what she did, the people she called friends and, most of all, her certainty about her future. Reminders of change poked her at every turn. She was surrounded by the sounds of an unfamiliar language and by landscapes that looked like paintings of a bygone era. Even the speed with which the ferry approached the Vila do Porto marina was different. She had gone from the hectic pace of life on the island of Manhattan to the exceedingly slow pace of life on the island of Santa Maria.

Lori stepped off the ferry. Sleep-deprived and disoriented, she blindly followed her fellow passengers along the dock. She could understand why Mr. Cardosa hadn't said exactly where in the marina he would meet her. Everything wasn't just slower; everything was smaller. She would be easy to spot in a population of mainly Mediterranean descent, a tall, sturdy blond dressed for an afternoon at the Metropolitan Museum ... not that there had been many of those in her twelve years in New York City. Weekends on the job had been mandatory to succeed in her business.

Everyone who disembarked with her was picked up by waiting friends or made their way into town on foot, and Lori soon found herself alone on the reception quay. She settled on a rickety wood bench in the shade of a large laurel tree and started to review the background material she had brought with her, the history and culture of an archipelago so isolated by thousands of miles of Atlantic Ocean that it wasn't even inhabited until the fifteenth century.

When she lifted her head to stretch her neck, she caught sight of herself in the window of the marina offices. *Norse Goddess, indeed. That face certainly doesn't fit the nickname they gave you.* Her eyes, such a pale golden gray that at times they seemed to match her hair, were bloodshot and drooped at the corners. Her fair skin, usually glowing and so fine-pored it looked air-brushed, had lost its color and been imprinted with fine lines. Lori combed back her thick hair and pinned it into a knot. Even if it was only a two-week assignment in a place few people had ever heard of, she intended to look as professional as she had on Madison Avenue.

Almost an hour passed, and Mr. Cardosa still had not appeared. The only activity was at the far end of the marina, where a gleaming white super-yacht, *Wit's End*, had docked, and Lori amused herself by doing what she did so well: she read people. She picked up on clues in their dress and vocabulary, and she interpreted body language and voice inflection. Those talents had been one reason for her success.

A shorter man in his fifties had a few words with the crew on deck before helping two men and two women onto dry land. Judging by his white uniform and cap, as well as by how the crew responded to him, Lori took him to be the Captain. He neatly tipped his cap to the four passengers and walked ahead of them to a shuttered window at the front of the small building near where Lori sat, the unseen observer.

A few seconds after he tapped on the window frame, the shutters were opened by a young man. "Bom día, Capitaó."

"Bom día to you," he replied, his pronunciation of the Portuguese greeting far worse than Lori, with absolutely no knowledge of the language, could have done. The man switched to English, and the two men quickly settled the details of berthing the yacht.

The four passengers caught up with the Captain. Lori knew their types well. She identified the leader of the group, carrying himself with confidence, a man used to controlling his world, probably a CEO or the owner of a successful company. Somewhat young for his type, he was in his late forties. He looked the picture of health, with a body that might have run to fat if not kept in check by the discipline of eating well and exercising regularly, probably in the executive gym. His lightly-defined muscles, tanned skin, and neatly trimmed light brown hair all confirmed that this was a man who took care of himself.

An immigrations official appeared at the window. "These are the papers for the crew, Capitaó Sullivan," he said, handing over a folder. "And these are the passengers?"

"Mr. Matthew Cunningham," Sullivan introduced the leader of the group, "and his wife, Mrs. Carolyn Cunningham." He took a step back. "If you don't mind, sir, immigrations has a few questions." The formality was intended to reflect both the status of the Cunninghams and the Captain's deference to them.

Cunningham pulled two American passports from an inside pocket of his windbreaker and handed them over. The official looked between the passports and the faces of the Cunninghams several times before stamping the documents on three pages.

The Captain then indicated the other two passengers. "Mr. Harold Stone and his wife, Mrs. Eleanor Stone."

At first glance, Matthew Cunningham and Harold Stone were physically alike, of about the same age and build, but behind the most obvious difference of Stone's darker features was a man far less at ease with himself and his position in life. From his carefully combed hair to his new clothes, this was someone trying hard to impress. His choice of words and the tone of his voice were designed to assert his superiority over others, probably because he had never reached the station in life he wanted so badly.

"Well, it seems like you have to jump through hoops to get into even tiny places like this," Harold Stone said, his condescension coming through a veil of friendliness so thin it wasn't meant to mask anything. "Ellie. The passports."

"You are Mr. Harold Stone?" asked the immigrations official as he leafed through the passports.

"That *is* my picture you're looking at." The chuckle was insincere.

He looked at the bleached blond next to Stone. "And you are Mrs. Eleanor Stone?"

Stone didn't wait for his wife to answer. "Yes," he drew the word out to show his impatience with a man too stupid to figure out the answer for himself. He looked to Matthew Cunningham for approval but didn't receive even a glance in return.

"Where have you come from?"

"New York last week, the Hamptons the week before. Right, Ellie?"

His wife seemed annoyed. "Yes."

The Captain stepped forward again. "Mr. Stone, his wife, and her sister, Mrs. Cunningham, came into Ponta Delgada aboard *Wit's End* on March 31st. Mr. Cunningham joined them two days later, and we set out for Santa Maria the following evening."

"Purpose of the visit?"

Stone said, "Business," at the same time that Cunningham said, "Pleasure."

"Yes," Stone said sourly, "A bit of both."

There was a long silence, followed by the stamping of official documents, before the Captain escorted his passengers away from the marina offices, crossing paths with a man who towered over all of them.

Anton arrived at the marina in record time. On the way, he had decided to talk over the morning's events with Catarina before settling on how much to tell Miss Moore. As he walked past the Americans standing near the docks to greet her, however, he heard a name that changed his mind. *Frank Dekker.* Somehow, he forced himself to keep putting one foot in front of the other and, in the space of just five seconds, he thought through his options. His English was poor, so circling back to listen to more of the conversation would not be the best choice. He would have to enlist Miss Moore's help.

Lori got up from the bench when she saw the tall man quickly closing the gap between them, his eyes fixed on her.

Anton desperately searched for the right English words. Without an introduction, he breathlessly said, "Help. Help to listen."

Her first response—so ingrained by city life it might as well have been an instinct—was a defensive, almost aggressive, posture.

"No. Go to listen." He raised his eyebrows and cocked his head in the direction of the Americans. "Please."

Lori would never know whether it was the desperation in his voice, her own curiosity, or simply that he looked so like an overgrown choir boy with his ruddy cheeks and puckish smile, but she felt her barriers dissolve.

As she turned towards the Cunninghams and the Stones, the man caught her by the shoulder. "Shh. Quiet. Very quiet," he said, putting a finger to his lips.

Lori nodded and headed in the direction of the Americans. She walked aimlessly in back of them, pretending to check her cell phone from time to time. The men were having a disagreement that would have been an argument had Stone not been working so hard to keep his temper in check and Cunningham not been so detached.

"I did not want to deal with Frank." Cunningham said with finality. His tone confirmed what Lori had determined about the man so far; he felt no need to persuade Stone.

"What about our investment?" There was deference in Stone's voice, but also fear.

"*Our* investment?"

"It will generate high returns if—" The rest was cut off by the sharp whistle of a boat in the harbor.

By the time Lori was able to hear the conversation again, Cunningham was saying, "—but I am still considering it." Stone only nodded but to Lori's observant eyes, he had also carefully exhaled the breath he was holding. He was relieved to know there was still a chance the investment would be supported by Cunningham.

A moment passed. The expression on Stone's face changed for the briefest moment, and Lori saw in him the same look that flickered on the faces of people who were about to play a winning hand. "Well, we both want what is best for our family." He emphasized the last word.

"Yes," replied Cunningham.

"What will we do about him?" Stone glanced in the direction of a young crewman, standing by the fuel pumps at the edge of the dock.

"I told you I would handle him."

The voices faded as the group moved forward to a waiting car. Lori knew following them would raise suspicions. Instead, she put on her dark glasses and faced the sea, looking sideways at the man Cunningham said he would *handle*. He was young and looked movie-star handsome, with rugged features and a deep golden tan that set off teeth so white, it was unlikely they were natural. He was in close conversation with a couple of young men, and Lori could tell he had them mesmerized. She could also tell he was trying to hide something.

Lori slowly walked back to where Anton waited. She stood silently looking at him until he bowed slightly and said, "Miss Moore."

"Mr. Cardosa." Lori extended her hand and smiled brightly, as she always did when meeting a new client.

2

Catarina Vanderhye had no time to watch the activity on the beach below Casa do Mar that morning. She was busy doing what made her happiest: being Anton's wife and the mother of their two children. More than any other consideration, the desire to have the best home for her family had brought her to Santa Maria.

As an advocate of family and community life, Catarina was very good. Even a casual observer might have come to that conclusion, for her appearance made one expect it. She had a gentle domesticity reminiscent of women in Vermeer paintings, perhaps a reflection of her Dutch heritage, and she carried with herself an air of serenity. She wore comfortable clothes, most often soft cotton shirts and loose pants that she covered with an apron when working around the house. She used no makeup, and she pulled her long hair into a bun before she even got out of bed in the morning. Still, when first meeting her, the overall impression a person got was one of femininity. She was gently-rounded and, even in her mid-forties, her titian hair was gloriously thick and shiny, her skin was flawless and rosy, and her lips were highly-colored.

Catarina was unpacking books when she heard Anton's old Volvo scatter gravel in the driveway that had been laid down the week before. She couldn't help but smile, knowing he was close by again. She put the carton of books in the storage room and turned her mind to making their guest feel welcome.

For Lori, the trip from the marina had been a harrowing drive along narrow roads that pitched uphill and down, scraping by other cars at high speed and with what seemed to be less than the space between her clenched teeth.

For Anton, the drive had been equally harrowing, but for a different reason. His mind had been crowded with a storm of thoughts. What should be done about the body found on the beach? How would this affect the meetings in two weeks? Should he just step back and postpone everything? The questions and answers chased each other. If he put everything in the hands of the police, that would leave the impact of Dekker's death beyond his control. If he assumed some responsibility for controlling the matter, that would associate a violent death more closely with his proposal. Either way, there could be negative fallout if the problem was not resolved before the participants arrived—but postponing the meetings might end his chances anyway.

He swerved into the driveway of Casa do Mar, the manifestation of everything he and Catarina wanted for their family and for their culture. Beside him, Lori grasped the door handle and took in a sharp breath as the car fell into what seemed to be empty space and swooped down towards a cliff set against a brilliantly blue ocean. Just before plummeting over the edge, Anton turned neatly into a small space below the grounds of Casa do Mar. He was a very good driver.

Lori managed a slight smile after she got out and steadied herself on wobbly legs.

"Come. Come," Anton motioned to her as his long legs carried him up the steep driveway. He swept an arm across the property. "Casa do Mar," he announced with pride. "Casa do Mar," he repeated, beaming.

They were at the foot of a grassy hill. To the west, a brook took a meandering course around enormous outcrops of volcanic rock and over small ones before disappearing into grove of flowering trees. To the east, neat rectangles made a patchwork in shades of green, each more intense that the last. A large barn and four smaller buildings, all constructed of black basalt stones set in limestone mortar, were scattered on the sloping meadow ahead.

Despite Anton's upturned mouth and bright eyes, Catarina could see the strain on her husband's face the moment he swung open the Dutch door to the kitchen. She went to him and wrapped her arms around his ample waist. Then she looked around him to Lori, who stood a few feet away, nearly drained of energy.

Anton turned to Lori and said, "The house. Come. Come." His English may have been limited, but he spoke it without a trace of embarrassment.

Catarina smiled, and in her smile was the welcome and the kindness needed to reassure Lori that she had not made a mistake in coming to Santa Maria.

"You are Lori Moore?" she asked in near-perfect English. "Please sit down. You must be very tired after your long trip. Would you care for some tea?" Her English reflected the formal setting in which she had learned it.

Lori gratefully took a seat and said, "Yes, please. A cup of tea would be very good right now."

An hour later, the three of them were still sitting around the well-worn oak table, and in that short time Lori had come to love Casa do Mar. Through the windows, she could see its emerald green hill spattered with bright wildflowers; though the open door, there was a 180° view of an enamel-blue sky capping an endless ocean. Warm breezes carried the faint scents of lavender and mint into the room, and she could hear ... well ... not much other than the sound of Catarina's soft, melodious voice. She felt very far from Manhattan.

With Catarina acting as interpreter, their conversation went slowly, but Lori loved the musical sounds of Portuguese, and thanks to her familiarity with romance languages, she even found herself picking up a few words and phrases.

Often finishing each other's sentences, the couple took turns laying out their vision for Casa do Mar and their proposal to the government of the Azores. Catarina told Lori how she and

Anton had invested all their money in a ten-acre property that had once been a dairy. She wanted to run it as a rural hotel that would allow her to work while still having time for her family. He wanted to showcase it as a model that would allow him to promote his ideas on cultural preservation. Their priorities were different, but each believed in both visions for the future.

The more ambitious part of their plan was to use private grants to purchase and conserve a large tract of land as a historic district. The central government would ensure the land was protected both environmentally and culturally, guaranteeing that everything from mills to vineyards to communal ovens would be used as they had been at various times in the island's past—a living model of Santa Maria's history.

They all shared a laugh over Anton's attempt to speak in English when he said, "Let Azores culture live!" but, although he may have sounded like just another passionate dreamer, he was far more. That was clear to Lori when he pulled meticulous research, projections, calculations, and even letters from political allies he had approached from a box of disorganized papers. He had a well-developed strategy and had been working toward it for years.

Anton's heart swelled when he found what had given him hope, the only positive response to the seventy-nine proposals he had written. He handed it to his wife, who passed it to Lori. It was written in English and addressed to Anton Luis Cabral Cardosa, Minister for Cultural Preservation, Autonomous Region of the Azores.

The Gillis Foundation has read your proposal with great interest. It is well in line with what John Gillis intended for his legacy. Mr. Calvin Wright and Miss Meghan Gillis will represent us and talk about your proposal. They will arrive in Ponta Delgada on the afternoon of April 18th and depart two days later. Kindly arrange transportation to Santa Maria. Details will follow.

Helping Anton and Catarina was right up Lori's alley. Controlling the nature and flow of information was what had made her a phenomenon. It was also what had cost her everything. She smiled. "Together we can present your proposal in the best light." And with that a remarkable alliance was forged.

As Lori looked over the grant requirements, Anton told his wife what had happened on the beach below Casa do Mar that morning. Lori read the exchanges between the married couple. She saw the moment when Catarina heard about the murder. She saw the sadness and the defeat that threatened both of them.

Then Anton told Catarina about what had taken place at the marina. She looked at him and shook her head, looking much like an exasperated mother who had caught her child being naughty again. "You asked our guest to spy on visitors?"

Anton raised his eyebrows even higher. "I had to, darling," he said apologetically.

Over the next half hour, as Lori examined paperwork and made notes, Anton turned to Catarina four times to ask what the American men had said about Frank Dekker. Each time, she said, "Let the girl finish what she is doing." He didn't challenge her. He knew she was always right when it came to people. Just as his desperation made him open his mouth a fifth time to shout, "Frank!" he heard his wife say the same name to Lori. He could tell Catarina was trying hard to make their guest understand that murder was not just rare on Santa Maria, it was unprecedented. When he heard the word *marina*, he focused all his attention on Lori.

Lori thought back to what she had overheard and pulled key words from her memory. Through Catarina, she told Anton about the disagreement between the man who appeared to be in charge and the man who deferred to him. She remembered that Cunningham had not wanted to work with Frank, and that Stone was very worried about an investment plan he wanted Cunningham to consider.

Anton was disappointed. What she had remembered resolved nothing.

The couple rose from their seats at the same moment. Without saying a word, Anton took the teapot to the stove, while Catarina filled the kettle with water. It was clear to Lori that, in addition to being devoted to one another, Anton and Catarina acted as a team in all parts of their lives.

Their cups refreshed, Lori recalled another part of the conversation between the two Americans at the marina, and she told Anton about how, after Stone mentioned wanting what was best for their family, Cunningham said he would handle the handsome young crewman by the fuel pumps. She also shared two insights: it was strange for a passenger to handle a problem with a member of the crew, and the crewman was hiding something.

Catarina explained that Anton feared an active murder investigation, especially one in full view of Casa do Mar, would present the island—and his entire proposal—in a negative light.

"We are looking at two different issues here," Lori said. "I know you're concerned about what happened this morning, but try to put the man on the beach—Frank—out of your mind for the moment. Although it's true that any association with a lack of safety might reflect negatively on Santa Maria and what you want to do, that is minor compared to everything else we have to deal with."

She waited for Catarina to translate, then took a deep breath and gave them the bad news. "I've read the expectations for a grant from the Gillis Foundation. We are going to need a miracle to make the best possible impression."

No translation was needed; it was clear Anton had understood. They were both stunned. Catarina's first thought was that her husband was going to be devastated. Anton's first thought was that he had let down his beloved wife. Their second thoughts were the same: they might have lost everything.

Anton was an optimist. It was in his nature to pay less attention to obstacles and more to possibilities. By the time they had finished their lunch of homemade vegetable soup and berry tart, warm from the oven, his faith in his plans had been restored. As they sipped espressos, he decided it was just that Lori didn't understand yet. *I must show her.* So, with renewed hope, he proudly led her to her bedroom at the far end of Casa do Mar's large barn for the nap Catarina had suggested. Along the way, he mapped out what he saw in each area, the three guest rooms people would enjoy coming home to, the small dining room where they would sample Catarina's home cooking, the comfortable living quarters for his own family.

What Lori saw as she followed Anton through the vast, dim space was far worse than she had anticipated: empty milking stalls, stacks of half-rotted stools, rusted tools, and mounds of decomposing hay. As far as she could see, there were only two areas even wired for electricity, the one with the kitchen and small bathroom, and—at the other end of barn—another that had been partitioned into three tiny bedrooms. Rather than needing some finishing touches to show its potential as a historic site, she realized Casa do Mar was derelict.

Far from being discouraged, however, the challenge of making Anton's vision a reality energized Lori. True, there was so much to do that the odds were against success, but just thinking about helping made her happier than she had been in a long time. By the time she drifted off to sleep, she had the framework of a plan in mind. After all, challenges like this had once been her specialty.

When Lori moved to New York after college, her intention was to become a journalist. Instead, she ended up in public relations at a large financial corporation, spinning information to convince investors their money would be safe, employees to work harder, and politicians to allow the firm free rein to continue operating as it had since it was founded in 1951.

She was smart, articulate, and likeable, and she had come into the field at a pivotal time, when the old media of newspapers, radio, and television were being replaced by digital media. She had seen the potential of cell phones, search engines, social media, and blogs, and had advanced quickly from writing copy for press releases to representing the company in key media outlets. When promoted to head the online presence group that was central to crisis intervention, she helped to craft the image that was essential to corporate success. In that capacity she was confronted with the expectation of manipulating perception, or—as most in her field called it—polishing the truth.

On those rare occasions when she thought about the nature of what she did for a living, Lori felt only vague dissatisfaction, which she usually resolved by reminding herself how fortunate she was to have a job such as hers, and she put aside her feelings—until one morning three weeks before arriving on Santa Maria.

An urgent communiqué appeared in her Inbox, followed within seconds by a phone call from the head of public relations. The corporation was about to lay off 20 percent of its workforce. She was asked to *cherry pick*—as the subject line of the email read— facts that would support the company's position that the reduction was regrettable but necessary, and then to disseminate euphemisms for how this would affect people. One of the email attachments Lori read was also sent to all employees who were to be laid off. Known as the justification, it explained how a loss of business and revenue necessitated laying off thousands of employees. It seemed straightforward. After all, a company shouldn't have to pay for work that didn't have to be done.

But social media is democratic. Theoretically, anyone can get their message out. By the time Lori finished scanning what was sent to her, someone had leaked the justification, and reactions in the anonymous posts that followed all said essentially the same thing: the company hadn't lost enough business to warrant such an action.

Lori was somewhat of a genius when it came to uncovering facts and figures, and the more she looked into it, the clearer it became that any lost business accounted for fewer than a hundred jobs. She realized that after the layoff, those who remained would simply be asked to take on more work, increasing their weekly hours to fifty and sixty and more. Legally, of course, overtime could not be mandatory, but the threat of job loss would be there, and they would do the work. Similarly, employees who had been laid off would be unwilling to lose severance packages with financial incentives that were contingent on not saying anything negative about the firm. There was little hope of anyone speaking up publicly.

Lori was more than smart, articulate, and likeable; she was also compassionate. Hoping to save people from the devastation of losing their jobs, she wrote up a faithful account of what she had uncovered and sent it out to media targets at 1:56 p.m. What the consequences might be for her never crossed her conscious mind. At 2:20 p.m., two security guards appeared at her desk, along with the Vice President for Human Resources. Her purse was checked before she was allowed to pick it up, and she was escorted to the parking lot, where the Vice President stood between her and her car, so angry he could barely catch his breath. Punctuating every word by stabbing a manicured finger into the air in front of her face, he said, "You ... will ... never ... work ... again."

She knew it wasn't true that she would never find another job, but she also knew what he meant. He would see to it that her prospects would be limited to work that did not require any reference to what she had done for twelve years. She had gone from the height of her profession to the possibility of not being able to find a clerical job.

Still dazed by the sudden change in her circumstances and everything that meant for her life, Lori looked through job postings that night. She spotted the most unsophisticated ad she had seen in many years. *B&B is looking for English speaker with public relations experience to write on ecotourism and culture on our lovely islands. Two-week assignment. Accommodations and food provided.* Only the smallest sum of money was offered, but she could use her frequent flyer miles and have a short vacation before resigning herself to an unappealing future.

By the time Lori re-appeared in the kitchen, the walls were covered with dreams. Sketches laid out the vision for Casa do Mar, with guest spaces and common areas labeled; watercolors showed comfortable rooms; and a map of Santa Maria showed large parts of the island preserved as historic trusts. Catarina had arranged Anton's papers into neat stacks, and left a pad of paper and two pencils ready for taking notes. Anton had gone through those stacks of paper, written a one-page summary of what each contained, and added that to the top of each pile. Both understood their roles.

Lori, too, understood her role. She would be the filter through which all their hopes and all their efforts would pass, to leave the best impression for the representatives from the Gillis Foundation. "You have both put together …," she started briskly but stopped herself. They weren't corporate clients; they were good people trying to do right by their family and their people. She started again, "I think what you are trying to do is …," she paused, trying to find the right word. The only one that came to mind was, "… admirable."

She picked up the letter from the Gillis Foundation. "By the time the representatives arrive at Casa do Mar, they will be tired and much of what you want to tell them they will have already heard many times before. All of the demands for their attention and their funding will have started to blend together in their minds." She directed her next words to Catarina. "First we must make them feel welcome and let them know we care about *them*, not just what they can give us."

"We are so far from the rest of the world," Catarina said, almost to herself, "it must first be worth their effort to come." She started a list of tasks.

After a short discussion, during which Anton agreed to clean out his car before driving the representatives around the island, Lori moved on. "Our biggest challenge will be to distinguish the Azores from every other place that wants to preserve its cultural heritage. Your visitors must understand the importance of what we are asking them to do. That is where you will shine, Anton. Talk to them as you did to me. Let them know how you see the future for your land *and* for your heritage."

Lori ended with an idea to show the visitors the potential of Casa do Mar itself. "Decision-makers like Mr. Wright and Miss Gillis know that the same passion they have for a cause can make an applicant blind to the realities of using grants effectively. We need to show them you would make exceptional use of what they gave you." In just two weeks, Lori wanted the shed at the far end of the property remodeled as a comfortable guest house that paid homage to the traditional architecture of the islands.

While Catarina went to get fresh fish for dinner and pick up the children from school, Anton and Lori continued with their action plans. Except for the tapping on keyboards and the occasional sigh, there was silence as they went about their work. As soon as Lori stopped to look out the window, however, Anton asked about what had been bothering him. "Frank dead no bad for Santa Maria?" He was looking for reassurance.

Lori didn't consider Anton's limited English when she replied. "There is no evidence the death would affect consideration by the Gillis Foundation." She was surprised to see him spring into action, first typing furiously on his laptop and then searching his pockets for a cell phone. She found it amusing that this man, who wanted to make sure that the culture of his ancestors was preserved so faithfully, actually carried three cell phones with him at all times, one provided by the government, one reserved for Casa do Mar business, and one his connection to Catarina.

Anton had heard the word *evidence*, so close to the Portuguese word *evidência*, and had assumed Lori needed information about the death before determining how it would affect consideration by the Gillis Foundation. Anxious to do as she asked, he called Felipe at the police station. "What did Dr. Leal say?" He knit his brows when he heard the response. "Okay. Send me the report," he said with some urgency.

Moments later, Anton heard the alert of a new email from his laptop. Knowing little English in a place that attracted tourists from America, Canada, and England had taught him how to use online translators. With a few keystrokes, he translated the attachment, and he turned his screen around to show Lori.

It was written in layman's terms and far shorter than Lori would have expected. Then again, she didn't know that Emanuel Leal had not examined a dead body since medical school, forty years earlier. In fact, he had consulted his old textbooks to do as much as he had done.

Francisco Dekker, 46 years of age
Resident of Ribeiras, Santa Maria
Found deceased at Farewell Beach
On the morning of April 4, 2015

A brief description of the body followed, with measurements, notes on a few old scars, and liver temperature. There were photographs of the wound on Frank's head, and a comparison between the wound and the bloodied rock found next to his body. With the exception tissue damage caused by the overconsumption of alcohol and decades of smoking, no other medical issues were noted. The one-page report ended with the doctor's brief conclusion.

Based on body and ambient temperatures, and on the
resolution of rigor, Francisco Dekker died between

approximately 21:00 and 23:00 on April 3, 2015. The position of the wound indicates it could not have been self-inflicted or the result of accident.

Lori was not concerned. Although news of a violent death would reach the island of São Miguel, where Mr. Wright and Miss Gillis were to enter the Azores, it was doubtful that either of them would be there long enough to even notice the headline, let alone know enough Portuguese to understand it. And once they were on Santa Maria, she would be able to control the information they were exposed to. That was, after all, her specialty.

On the other hand, Anton was more worried than ever. As he read Dr. Leal's report, some part of his mind, one that operated below the level of consciousness, had picked up on a fact that troubled him. He was now convinced that the murder was significant to the proposal he was asking the Gillis Foundation to accept; he just couldn't pinpoint why. He said, "Americans in marina talk Frank."

"Yes," Lori replied slowly. She wasn't sure where he was going with his thought.

"Americans in marina …," Anton took a handful of coins from his pocket, put them on the table, and continued, "… much, much Euros."

"The Americans at the marina had a lot of money." Lori understood what he was saying, but she still had no idea why it was so important to him.

Anton nodded vigorously. Then he shuffled through the papers on the table, upsetting every pile Catarina had made, and pointed to the one from the Gillis Foundation. He questioned Lori with his eyes. "Little Americans …," he counted on his fingers, "… one, two, three Americans in Vila do Porto marina abril." He remembered words Lori had just used. "Americans at marina a lot of money and in Vila do Porto abril."

Lori understood. He wanted to tell her that very few Americans came into Santa Maria aboard boats in April, and these were very wealthy ones. He was worried that Cunningham's group of travelers was associated with the Gillis Foundation, and that they had already heard about Frank's death and found it significant. She nodded. That could be a problem.

An idea occurred to Anton. The immigration forms that visitors fill out ask for occupations. He signaled Lori to wait while he made a call on the newest of his three cell phones, the one issued to him as a minister of the central government. He hoped that by speaking with enough authority, he could persuade someone to find the forms and tell him what was written on them.

"This is Minister Anton Cardosa. Who is speaking?" he said crisply. "A group of Americans came in by boat yesterday. I want to know their names and occupations."

The person who answered the call told him the office was just closing for the day. He would leave a note for his supervisor to read in the morning.

Anton used the same line he had used with the police officers that morning. "You will find that information now! Your job depends on it." A few minutes passed before Anton wrote the names that the immigrations officer slowly spelled out for him: Matthew Cunningham, Carolyn Cunningham, Harold Stone, Eleanor Stone. Anton exhaled deeply when he heard they were not employed by the Gillis Foundation. His relief was short-lived.

Anton had his way of gathering information, and Lori had hers. While he was on the phone, she did what she had done so many times as a public relations specialist: she searched for Cunningham and Stone on LinkedIn. True, they were not with the Gillis Foundation; their firm did, however, invest heavily in vacation resorts and in recent months, it had publicly promoted its intention to move into lesser known markets. Lori remembered how Cunningham and Stone had given different reasons for the purpose of their visit.

Was it business or pleasure? And why were they on Santa Maria at the same time that the representatives from the Gillis Foundation were expected?

Liliana was intrigued by the American visitor. Ten years old, she was a serious child who took after her mother in mannerisms and speech. Her shy smile was a perfect match for Catarina's, her hair and thoughtful eyes were dark like her father's, and her skin was a striking blend of Northern European rosiness and Southern European gold.

She took a seat next to Lori and observed her carefully, noting the way she held her body, strong and relaxed at the same time, and her clothes, especially the pastel blue shirt that looked so soft, the child thought it would feel like touching a cloud. Most of all, she could not stop looking at her long hair, gleaming like polished gold in the late-afternoon sun.

Her English was very good. "Mama has been teaching me," she said. "One day I am going to university in England."

Catarina felt a small stab to her heart. She never liked thinking of the day when her children would be away from her, living other lives.

Toni was named after his father, and their bond was clear. Moments after Anton came into the kitchen, he lifted the seven-year-old high in the air. Masses of reddish-brown curls topped a face that still held its child's features, fine-pored light olive skin, large brown eyes, and a cherub's red mouth that matched Anton's. They had eyes only for each other until Catarina reminded both of them that Toni had not yet greeted Lori. He, too, spoke English—although not quite as well as his sister—and when Lori complimented him on it, Anton's personality came through. "Of course," he grinned broadly, "Papa is the only one here who does not speak English." He wagged a small finger at his father, "He must learn now!"

"Ah," boomed Anton fiendishly, "I need a teacher." And with that, he captured Toni in his arms and carried him away.

A flurry of activity accompanied the children home. They settled at the kitchen table, first for a snack—since even for children, dinner was eaten late in the evening—and then to do their homework under Catarina's watchful eye. Lori enjoyed helping them with English homework, especially when she saw the pride on their faces every time they answered correctly. While Liliana finished a geography assignment, Toni was sent in search of eggs to make the custard for dessert. He started out the door, but returned, brought his child's face close to Lori's, and asked, "You will like to come with me to get eggs?"

Two hours later, all homework was done, the custard was cooling, the goats had been visited, and Anton had led them all in practicing football—or as Lori knew it, soccer—kicks. It was as happy a group as Lori had ever been part of. Liliana and Toni disappeared for baths on their own accord, and returned for dinner, which was delicious. A stew with kale from the garden and fleshy white beans that had been soaking all day was followed by Catarina's custard—or "celebrity custard," as Anton put it. Liliana explained that her father said the custard was so good, it was famous.

When the time came for the children to go to bed, everyone took a flashlight from a shelf by the kitchen door and made their way through what had become a pitch black cavernous space, scanning the floor for coils of rope, milk pails, and rotting stools as they went. Both children were tucked into Toni's bed, since their guest had Liliana's room during her visit. Lori stayed while Catarina read a few pages from *The Wind in the Willows* to them. She was a gifted storyteller, speaking in a different voice for each character, and she had the attention of one and all.

Anton took one last look at his family before the adults made their way back to the kitchen. He wished his parents had been able to see how his life had turned out. He wished they could have known they would have such precious grandchildren. Catarina read her husband's face. She, too, thought of her parents and wished they had not made the choices they did, and could have known Liliana and Toni as they grew.

The birds had sung their last evening songs, the children were asleep at the other end of the old dairy building, and the adults were sipping espressos. It had been a long day for all three of them. Anton went to close the upper panel of the kitchen's Dutch door and looked out at the night sky.

"Come see," Catarina whispered to Lori. "People who visit the islands from America love this." She turned out the kitchen lights and guided her to the door.

Lori could not breathe. Here, above an island in a black ocean far from Europe and the Americas, was a starscape so spectacular no picture she had ever seen, no description she had ever read, had prepared her for it. Uncountable pinpricks of light made a brilliant gossamer curtain that lined the vast dome overhead. She could understand why Man had always thought of heaven in the skies.

She closed her eyes. *Make a memory. You will never see such a sight again. Make a memory.*

Anton looked at Lori's face, caught in a moment of rapture. His eyes met Catarina's, and they smiled at each other. Each knew what the other was thinking, and each was thinking the same thing. *What we have is special. What we have is worth the fight.*

It was then that it dawned on Anton exactly what had disturbed him when he read Dr. Leal's report. It was the name: Francisco Dekker. Dutch names were not unusual in an archipelago that once had so many Flemish settlers they were known as the Isles of Flanders, but Dekker was not a common one. Anton had the feeling he had heard it before—and in connection with Casa do Mar.

Heart pounding, he flipped on the kitchen lights.

"What's wrong?" asked his wife, for she knew something was wrong.

Bewildered, Lori and Catarina watched as he grabbed his battered book bag. Catarina had given it to him. It was arguably his most treasured possession. It showed her faith in him when he had little in himself. It was an emblem of a changed life.

He frantically rummaged through papers looking for the title to all the coastal land that adjoined Casa do Mar to the west, the land that the Gillis Foundation and the central government were being asked to help conserve. Matias Costa, one of the two owners of the land and a longtime advocate of the movement to preserve the traditions of the Azores, had enthusiastically agreed to the sale of the property. He had also assured Anton that the other owner accepted the terms of sale—in fact wanted nothing more than to make his profit and move away.

The second owner was Francisco Dekker.

3

Over the years, Catarina had become used to her husband's late hours, and she rarely even stirred when he came to bed. She enjoyed the first few solitary hours of the day, watching dawn break and nature come back to life while she sipped her milky coffee. It came as a surprise then to find his side of the bed empty when she woke up, and her first thought was that something was wrong. She dressed quickly and walked through the old barn, still in shades of pearly gray in the early-morning light.

The kitchen looked exactly as it had when she and Lori left Anton to his paperwork the night before, so she took her shawl from a hook by the Dutch door and went to look around Casa do Mar. Long before she could hear him, she saw her Anton walking with Lori and pointing with pride to each building and tree and rock. She knew exactly what he was saying, the same words she had heard when he first brought her to this place, the words his children hung on like a favorite story, the words he hoped would help the Gillis Foundation to understand his vision.

When she joined them by the fallen walls of an old chapel, Anton handed her the outcome of his all-night effort. It was a printed list of tasks for the day, some tagged with his name, some with Lori's, and some with hers. Lori was going with Anton to get some information on Santa Maria from his office, and then spending the rest of the day working on presentation materials for the Gillis Foundation. Catarina was going to order the furnishings for their first guest house and to ask the mother of one of Toni's classmates, the best photographer on the island, to take pictures before, during, and after the restoration. Anton was going to hire masons, plumbers, and electricians, and return in time to start them on their work that afternoon.

At least that was the plan.

Anton simply could not resist. He shot up the driveway but instead of turning right to go directly to Vila do Porto, he turned left. *What harm could there be in showing Lori a bit of Santa Maria?* The long way around led to a tour of the little island, only 5 miles wide and 10 miles long, narrated in Anton's best attempts at English and many expansive gestures. *Ah!* was his favorite thing to say, accompanied by a broad smile, as he pointed here and there along the way.

Lori saw rapidly changing vistas: deep green forests of soaring cedars; sunlit meadows; cactus-speckled red deserts; shallow valleys dotted with grazing cows; pristine bays; and miles of hillsides lavender with hydrangeas, purple with oleanders, and pink with rhododendrons. Remnants of tall volcanoes fell into hills and river valleys before ending at the cliffs that rimmed the island, just as by Casa do Mar. Footpaths led to beaches enclosed by spectacular headlands, empty even on the warm spring day. At the shore, she saw sand of different colors—white, gold, and black—and water that varied from so placid it didn't appear to move at all to pounding surf.

Anton sped along the narrow roads, beeping and waving at the people he occasionally passed along the way. He stopped only once to show her the tiny chapel in Anjos, where Columbus had given thanks on his return voyage from the New World. Not a single tourist was in sight.

It was late morning before they arrived in the main town of Vila do Porto, resting on a hillside that rolled down to the sea. With fewer than 3,000 inhabitants, it was nearly as quiet as every other place on the island. Anton took his visitor past small squares shaded by palm trees, old whitewashed churches, and charming houses with wrought iron balconies, driving over the old cobblestones as quickly as he had on the paved highways. By the time he stopped in the middle of a road, every part of Lori's body had been jarred. He indicated that she should get out, and then pulled up onto the narrow sidewalk, leaving about an inch of space between the passenger side door and the building, which served as Santa Maria's city hall, police station, and post office. Anton had an office there, and he intended to ask the people he had come to know about the best workers for the restoration at Casa do Mar.

It seemed everyone knew Anton. With friendly waves and greetings from people walking by, it took ten minutes before they could even climb the steep steps to the front door. Once inside, there was much the same delay as outside; from the woman who was carrying tea into an office to the man who was cleaning windows, everyone who caught sight of Anton was drawn to his smiling face. Each time, he introduced Lori and then exchanged a few words with his people. She had to admire his magnetism. *If this were America, he'd be running for political office. And he'd win.*

Once inside his office, Anton showed Lori the letter from Presidente Moniz that was on his desk. "Yes. Me, Anton Luis Cabral Cardosa," he said, pointing to the words. "Mi-nis-ter," he said slowly in English.

He was so solicitous of Lori's comfort, offering her water, adjusting the blinds to screen her from the high sun, bringing her a stack of picture books and brochures on the islands, she was glad when he finally settled down. She saw his business side when he made nine phone calls in rapid succession, ticking off points on a folded list he had taken from his pants pocket and adding new notes to the page. *He's far more than a jovial bear of a man,* she thought.

She gathered that someone named Beto would arrive at Casa do Mar after lunch, as would a mason, an electrician, and a plumber. Plants—"very colorful and large enough to look like they had been there for ten years"—were ordered, and a print shop on São Miguel was put on standby for "a very special order." Lori knew at once who received the last call; Anton's voice was different, mild and affectionate, as he told Catarina about what he had done and who to expect.

Just as they stood to leave, Felipe came in. When he saw Lori, he stopped short. "I'll come back, sir."

Anton waved him in and introduced Lori. Felipe had to stand on tiptoes to give her the traditional two kisses on the cheek, adding a third when he saw the three fingers Anton held up.

Lori couldn't wait to ask Catarina what that was about.

Felipe started backing away, again saying, "I'll come back, sir."

Anton turned to Lori. "Felipe and Anton talk. You sit? Okay?"

Lori assured him that was fine and settled back with the reading he had given her.

Felipe glanced at Lori and said very quietly, "Sir, since Chief Tavares is away, should we call someone about Frank's death?"

The question was not unexpected. Anton had wondered the same thing several times. Under normal circumstances, the head of police taking three weeks to visit relatives in America was barely worth noting. These, however, were not normal circumstances. Above all, Anton didn't want to attract the attention that might follow a call to the Judicial Police in Ponta Delgada. "First, we must ask ourselves, what good will come of such a call," he said, hoping it didn't seem like he wanted a cover-up. "What is it we need from them?"

"Well, sir, we don't know what should be done with ...," his voice dropped to a whisper, "... Frank." Felipe was of an older generation, and he held that women were to be protected from the harsher things in life. The truth was that many of the younger men on the island shared that sentiment. "He's still ...." He looked down at the floor to remind Anton that the body was in the basement below them.

Anton exhaled loudly enough for Lori to look up. "If Dr. Leal is finished, I will ask Frank's family what is to be done." A moment later, he added, "Who is his family?"

Just as at the beach, he was faced with a surprised look. "Isabella. From Water's Edge."

"Isabella is his wife?"

Felipe nodded.

"And where is Water's Edge? And *what* is Water's Edge?"

"Water's Edge is on the other side of Farewell Beach—your beach. At the top of the cliff opposite Casa do Mar."

Just above where Frank was found, thought Anton.

"It's ... well, it's Water's Edge. It's ...," he searched for the right way to describe it, "... where the fishermen go before setting out. It's where their families go while waiting for them to return. It's a bar and a café and a restaurant—,"

Felipe seemed almost grateful when Anton interrupted him. "Where are Frank's belongings?"

Felipe returned less than a minute later with a large brown paper bag. "His clothes are in here. There was no money in his pockets, nothing but ...," he fished around in the bag, "... this."

It was part of a page torn from an American magazine. On one side, *Oprah's Favorite Things* showed a picnic basket at $600 and the top half of a collection of scented candles, price unknown. In the white space on the other side, someone had written in English.

April 4th
Vila do Porto marina
Wit's End
<u>*Both of you.*</u>

Water's Edge had changed quite a bit since Lourens Dekker and Manoel Costa stacked the first basalt stones against a rocky outcrop. For one thing, back then it did not carry that name—or indeed any name. It was just a place near the water's edge where fishermen could warm themselves with local wine before setting off for weeks at sea, or where parents met the American whaling men and—to avoid riskier military conscription—handed over their young sons, never to see them again.

The first Dekker to own Water's Edge was the son of a hard-working wheat farmer who had died young; the first Costa was the son of a whaler who had died at sea. Both dreamed of better lives for themselves and their families. They met one evening and, over bottles of wine, talked about a future as vintners. They did everything right. They spent ten years planning before they made a move. They calculated all costs and saved money, not easy on an island where almost everyone was on the brink of dire poverty. They surveyed the island for the best place for their vineyards.

Finally, they bought land that stretched for two miles along the rocky coast and one mile inland. Exposed to scraping winds that came off the Atlantic, their land was not considered good for farming, but the two were going to plant vineyards in the traditional way. For almost two years, they left their blood on the stones they cleared from small patches of ground and used to terrace the hillside with low walls that could shelter the plants from the cool salt air.

The same year they bought the land, however, a disease appeared and by the time they harvested the first grapes, it was hard to find a vine on any of the islands that did not show signs of rot. Water's Edge was intended to be a place where they could sell the little wine they did make and survive until the vines recovered. They never did.

One hundred and fifty years later, there was a painted sign over the door, not because it was needed but because the Costa and the Dekker of the last generation had felt such pride of ownership in their legacy. As his father before him, Carlos Costa had a talent for carving wood, so he fashioned a bas relief that captured the cliff where Water's Edge was situated. And, as his father before him, Leandro Dekker had a talent for painting, so he added the blues of the ocean and sky, the greens of the grass and the trees, and—in bright white—the name *Water's Edge*. As they hung the sign, both men talked about how they looked forward to passing on what they had been given to their infant sons.

Anton and Lori walked into a very different place than the one where patrons sat on wood crates and brought their own candles to light the way. For one thing, it was now three rooms, two of them added as the prosperity of the owners grew over the years. The oldest rooms had small windows and unfinished walls, and it was understood by all that they were where rough language and hard drinking were to be sequestered. No one in the community wanted women or children or priests exposed to such things.

The newest and largest of the rooms had been made welcoming by Frank Dekker's wife, Isabella. The walls were lined with planks of wood recovered from a ship that had run aground just offshore in the 1920s, banquettes were upholstered in restful shades of green, and framed pictures told the story of Water's Edge. A fire burned on the patio outside, scenting the air with woodsmoke and wrapping everything with a warm glow at night.

Isabella looked like she had been type-cast as the siren in a 1950s film. Her wavy hair was a rich brown, like her wide-set eyes, and her lips were full and red. She even moved her shapely body sinuously as she wiped down table tops. "What can I do for you?" she asked. Her voice was a surprise, not deep as one might expect, almost that of a child.

Lori quietly stepped back. In that setting, she knew she was limited to being an observer, and she was well suited to that role. Her familiarity with other romance languages allowed her to follow much of what was said well enough and—freed from participating in the conversation—her talent reading body language actually gave her a greater understanding than most people who were fluent in Portuguese would have had.

Anton composed himself, then said, "I need to speak with Francisco Dekker's wife."

Isabella blanched and put a hand on the back of a chair. She seemed to steel herself for something unpleasant when she said, "I am Frank's wife."

A man had appeared in the doorway to one of the back rooms. "I am Manuel Dekker, Frank's brother," he said gruffly. Lori could see how quickly and tightly he closed his jaw after he spoke; the man was trying hard to control himself. He walked quickly to Isabella's side.

An image of what he had seen on the beach the day before flashed in Anton's mind. The man had a strong family resemblance to Frank, the same compact body, the same reddish hair and large brown eyes. His eyes on Isabella, Manuel pulled out a chair for her.

Again, Anton found himself having to do what he thought he would never be able to do, or at least to do well. At first, he tried to recall how his wife's favorite detectives delivered such news, but ultimately he found he was confident enough to simply say what he thought was best. "I am sorry, truly sorry, to tell you that your husband is dead." He gave Frank's widow and his brother very few details when he explained what had happened, and they did not press him for any information. In fact, neither seemed terribly upset by the news. Manuel said he would arrange for the body to be picked up and cremated; and, when Anton explained that the police would be holding Frank's belongings for a while longer, both said that there was no need to return them. The victim did not seem to be a man who would be missed by his family.

"Paolo," Isabella murmured. She withdrew into her own thoughts and was quiet for long moments. Then she narrowed her eyes and repeated, "Paolo," in her childlike voice, this time with surprising determination.

"Who is Paolo?" Anton asked gently.

Manuel stepped behind Isabella and put his hands on her shoulders. "Paolo is Isabella's son. He is only eight and with friends now."

Isabella nodded slowly, still thinking. She turned her large almond eyes to Manuel, and they exchanged slow, knowing nods. Lori could see the smallest of smiles flicker on the woman's face.

Manuel drew himself up with a look of pride, "Paolo is the next Dekker; he now owns half of Water's Edge."

"And you are the other owner?"

To Lori's ears, Manuel's small laugh was tinged with bitterness. "No. The other owner will be back soon. He is just bringing the evening's bread from the bakery."

Anton was about to ask the name of the other man who owned Water's Edge, but that became clear to him the moment the front door opened. A handsome, middle-aged man with solemn eyes walked into the room carrying an enormous basket filled with freshly baked bread. Anton's eyebrows lifted even higher than usual, and he gave a barely audible gasp. "Matias," he said. Dekker's partner in Water's Edge was Matias Costa, the same man who had agreed to sell his share of the land that Anton's plan depended on, the same man who had told him that Francisco Dekker would also agree to sell his share.

Matias put the basket of bread on the nearest table, smiled broadly, and extended his hand to Anton. Hoping Lori would remember, Anton turned to her and said in wobbly English, "This is Matias *Costa*. Talk about Matias last night."

Lori smiled and again was given three kisses—left, right, left—as by Felipe at the police station. All the while, she and Anton were thinking the same thing. *Frank Dekker's death could very well ruin what they were working towards.*

Anton took a nearly hidden road that clung to the edge of a cliff. Lori decided to save herself the fear of plummeting over the side of the mountain by keeping her eyes closed until Anton pulled the car to the side of the road. He extracted himself from the car, raced to the passenger side, and held the door open for Lori, smiling as brightly as he had when he lifted little Toni high overhead the day before. "Mmm," he said, gathering his fingertips to his nose and inhaling deeply. "Come. Come." Lori needed no encouragement; with the aromas of butter and garlic and baking bread in the air, she was already salivating.

She followed him into a house set in a grove of trees, some of which leaned almost horizontally over the ocean a hundred feet below. His head barely cleared the door frame—in fact, his body barely cleared the small doorway. Other than his own kitchen, this was Anton's favorite place to eat. In just four weeks back on Santa Maria, he had made himself very much at home there. After settling Lori at one of the four tables overlooking the sparkling blue water, he went to greet the only other people in the restaurant, two men playing a game of dominoes. Then, tunefully humming to himself, he went in search of Alicia.

He returned with a basket of fresh bread, a bowl of warm olive oil speckled with herbs, and a bottle of wine tucked under one arm. He took the seat opposite Lori and opened the bottle with the corkscrew that was on the table. Despite Catarina's excellent dinner the night before, Lori was famished. She remembered her reaction in those first days after being marched out of the office in disgrace, unlikely to ever be well-employed again. *I'm making up for what I didn't eat before I left!*

They both sat in silence, looking at the view, not thinking about much at all. Just as Anton poured second glasses of wine, Alicia appeared carrying two plates, each with an enormous piece of grilled tuna sitting on a sauce of chopped tomatoes, minced garlic, and capers. "I hope you will like this," she said to Lori. Like many on Santa Maria, she spoke English well.

"It looks delicious. Fresh fish is a real treat for me."

"You cannot get much fresher. This morning, it was swimming out there," she looked through the window at the cove at the base of the cliff.

Anton's favorite lunch tasted even better watching Lori's pleasure as she cleaned her plate with the last piece of bread. They didn't speak a word until after Alicia left them with their espressos. Then Anton said, "Go to marina? To boat? You talk to

Americans?" He pulled out the paper the police had found in Frank's pocket and handed it to her. Mostly because he wanted it to be true, he was holding on to the belief that the killer was someone from the outside. *A Mariense could not have killed one of its own.*

Lori wasn't at all clear why Anton, a businessman and a government minister charged with protecting the national heritage, played any role in investigating Frank Dekker's death. In fact, the thought of him as a detective amused her almost as much as the thought of helping him to be a detective. *Well, it's a far cry from working at a Madison Avenue desk.* She was beginning to understand his concern, almost his preoccupation, with finding out what had happened on the beach below Casa do Mar. He was doing everything he possibly could to ensure that his dreams, and Catarina's dreams, became reality. With information organized, with masons hard at work, electricians and plumbers hired, plants ordered, photographs arranged for, and glossy packets of information planned, the one thing left for him to do was to make sure murder did not taint all their efforts.

Lori was only partly correct. The rest of the truth, one that Anton was just beginning to admit to himself, was that he rather enjoyed the idea of being a bit like one of Catarina's British detectives.

At the marina, it had only taken a glance at Anton's government identification card for the *Wit's End* crewman on duty to escort them up the gangplank.

"What do you want?" Harold Stone called out, leaning over the railing of the main deck.

Lori kept a steady pace and assumed the face she had always worn when she dealt with the press or the Board of Directors about a difficult matter, a face intended to give the impression that she was in control of the situation.

Anton followed, his heart beating a bit fast—whether from seeing the lavishness of a luxury yacht or from looking forward to acting as a detective, he couldn't say.

By the time they reached the main deck, the largest and most luxurious of the three decks they saw, Matthew Cunningham had joined Stone and both men stood waiting for them.

"This is a private yacht," Stone said.

Lori ignored him, turned to Anton, and said deferentially, "Minister Cardosa. Please go ahead." Anton followed her lead and nodded somberly, trying to keep the grin that threatened in check.

Starting to have fun with this herself, Lori extended her arm toward Anton, made the slightest of bows, and said, "Your Excellency, I would like to introduce Mr. Harold Stone and Mr. Matthew Cunningham." It all seemed so official, the two American men didn't even question how she knew their names.

She continued, "This is Minister Anton Cardosa of the Autonomous Region of the Azores. I am Lori Moore. I am here as Minister Cardosa's interpreter." With Anton's exclamations, nods, and usual grin, anyone would have assumed that he was an active participant in what followed. In truth, Lori took the lead in the conversation, prompted only occasionally by Anton's broken English and hand gestures, which she found she was beginning to understand quite well.

Cunningham's sharp green eyes assessed the situation quickly. Having had such little control over his circumstances when he was a child, he had worked hard to have control over his circumstances as an adult. He was savvy enough, however, to know when not to exercise that control. "We can talk in the salon," he said.

In an apparent change of heart about their visit, Stone asked that they call him Harry and began to give a tour of the room. He used remote controls to slide retractable doors into paneled tigerwood walls and to fold a large screen television up to the ebony ceiling. Even the bar was adjustable, descending into the floor. "So we have room to dance the night away," he flirted with

Lori. He pointed to a winding teak staircase that accessed a steam room and gym.

Even Lori, who had been invited to events on such yachts berthed at docks in Manhattan, was impressed with the space. It was easily more luxurious than most upscale homes on land would have been. She checked Anton's reaction to what they saw, but the only change she could detect was a slight widening of his eyes.

Cunningham introduced them to his wife and Stone's, both lounging on white leather sofas at the far end of the salon. Neither did more than to look up briefly and give their visitors weak nods before returning to their magazines.

"What can I do for you?" asked Cunningham.

"Minister Cardosa has a few questions." She swept the salon with her eyes to indicate that she was including all of them.

"About what exactly?" asked Stone.

"A resident of Santa Maria has been found dead."

"What makes you think we know anything about the death of some local figure?" Stone challenged Lori.

She continued as though she hadn't even heard him. "In light of your status as visitors to Santa Maria, the Minister will ask a few questions before determining whether or not to involve you in an interrogation by the police." She had chosen her words carefully. She was well aware that *you* could refer to anyone in the room, and she carefully kept moving her gaze from one to another as she spoke.

Stone cut her off. "We only arrived yesterday, hardly enough time to make enemies, or even friends."

"It is known to the police that he had an appointment here on April 4th." She used the vaguest term to describe the meeting. *Here*, after all, could be anywhere from the room in which they sat to the entire island.

Cunningham's response was simple. "I had no plans to meet anyone on April 4th." He was as adept at using language to lead someone astray as Lori was—and she could see that. She also sensed that he was either withholding information or lying outright.

"Mrs. Cunningham?" She looked up, but appeared puzzled. "Did you know him?" she clarified. Carolyn Cunningham was still not processing the question. Up to this point, Lori had avoided mentioning Frank by name, hoping someone else would. *Just like a real detective.* It hadn't worked, so she asked again, "Did you know Mr. Dekker?"

"Dekker?" She looked at her sister, baffled. "Is he the one from the boat?"

Almost imperceptibly, Eleanor Stone shook her head.

"I miss him," said Carolyn Cunningham. "We really need to bring him back."

A few moments of silence passed. Lori repeated her question. "Did you know Mr. Dekker?"

This time she answered, "No."

"And you know nothing of an appointment he had?"

"No."

"Mrs. Stone?"

She had been staring at her magazine, but it was clear she had also been listening closely. "No to both questions." Lori knew short, firm answers such as those were often used to end any further exploration of an answer but more than that, Eleanor Stone was unreadable.

"And you, Mr. Stone?" The change in Stone's face in the sixty or so seconds since she had last looked at him was small but significant. He was paler, and the artery pulsing in his neck told her his heart was racing.

He looked at Cunningham before answering, whether for guidance or approval or something else, Lori couldn't tell, and his mouth was dry when he said, "I have no connection with anyone on this island."

Anton could see no one had owned up to knowing Frank Dekker. He reached into his pocket for the paper that had been found on Frank's body but changed his mind when he remembered a scene from a mystery show he had watched with Catarina. He decided to hold back something until everyone associated with *Wit's End* had said as much as they would. Then, perhaps, that small scrap of paper could be used as evidence that someone had lied.

Lori had seen Anton start to pull the paper from his pocket and then stop. She picked up on the barely noticeable shake of his head and changed what she was going to say. "We would like to talk to the Captain now." She wasn't going to thank them or let them think that was the end of the matter.

Stone escorted them to the pilothouse and stayed in the doorway watching. "Go ahead. Don't mind me."

Captain Sullivan never allowed himself to be referred to as anything other than *Captain*, and very few people even knew his first name. That fact, along with the scar on his broad forehead, made him look somewhat fiercer than he was and made the crew fear his wrath more than was warranted. On the shorter side, he was comfortably padded and his crisp white shirt overhung his polished belt just a bit. The hair on his head had long since given way to baldness, but he sported a bristly white mustache and shrewd blue eyes that looked out from under a ledge of bushy white eyebrows.

When Lori wanted to make an ally, whether of the press or of the competition, she started with friendly admiration of what the person did. She looked at all the blinking lights on the monitors and said, "This looks more like the console of a jet fighter plane than a boat."

"She's not just a coast-hugger," he said with pride. "Her tanks hold 1200 gallons of fuel, reverse osmosis makes 1600 gallons of fresh water a day from seawater, and this beauty is fire resistant from the woods to the carpets."

"That's a lot to oversee," Lori commented.

"He does have help," Stone interjected.

The Captain frowned at him and said to Lori, "She has monitors for the generators, fuel tanks, water levels, and so much more." Then, perhaps more pointedly than warranted, he added, "I know *everything* that happens on her."

Stone tried to reclaim the conversation. "It's the best money can buy."

Lori saw the Captain wince when *Wit's End* was referred to as *it*. "If *she* has a problem, an automatic alert is sent out—,"

Stone interrupted, "—to my iPhone." Almost an afterthought, he added, "And the Captain's, of course."

The Captain's eyes rolled. "I can even pilot *Wit's End* from any deck." He turned to Stone and added with exaggerated deference, "And of course, you can, too, sir."

Lori judged they had spent enough time on pleasantries. "I am Lori Moore, and I am here to translate for his Excellency Mr. Cardosa, Minister Plenipotentiary of the Autonomous Government of the Azores. She was making things up as she went along and had no idea whether the titles she used were even correct. She did know she enjoyed seeing the effect her words had on the Captain.

She asked the same questions she had asked in the salon, and essentially she got the same responses. "Do you know Francisco Dekker?"

Captain Sullivan blinked twice and said, "I don't know a Francisco Dekker."

"Do you know about a meeting with him?" Behind her, Stone loudly shifted position.

Sullivan laughed, "I'm a ship's captain not a businessman. The only people I meet with are my crew and the Cunninghams."

He seemed honest, but Lori wondered about the telltale blinking—and she was well aware that the worst of people could be skilled liars.

A door at the rear of the pilothouse opened, and Lori could see into a small bedroom, presumably the Captain's. A slightly built girl in her late teens stood in the doorway, swaying unsteadily. She looked like she had just woken from a troubled sleep. Her shorts and shirt were badly rumpled, and her thick, dark hair was in complete disarray, long strands tangled and matted around her shoulders. Her eyelids were barely lifted, but Lori could see that her pale grey eyes were bloodshot and glassy. She looked only at the Captain, who took two long steps across the room to reach her quickly. He wrapped an arm firmly around the girl's waist, turned her around, and laid her down in the bunk, where she immediately curled into a ball and fell asleep.

After he had closed the door and returned to them, Lori asked, "Is she alright?"

The Captain didn't make eye contact. He just mumbled, "My daughter. She's sick."

Clearly, he was uncomfortable talking about it, and she decided to let it go. Anton cleared his throat. When Lori looked at him, he pointedly stared out the window at a women wiping down deck chairs. It took her a moment to follow his gaze and understand what he was trying to tell her.

"We would like to question the crew," she said to the Captain.

"Easy enough. They're all at their duty stations right now." He picked up a handset and his words were broadcast throughout the ship. "All crew to quarters. All crew to quarters."

Stone spoke up, more loudly than was needed in such a small space, "I'll meet you down there," and with that he walked away.

The Captain led Anton and Lori down a different staircase than the one they had taken to the main deck. At the bottom, he pointed out a swim step, complete with a shower, diving equipment, and outlets to re-fill air tanks, and then he walked them through a modern galley to the crew quarters, where Stone waited for them. Eleven men and six women stood in six rooms outfitted with narrow bunks, each personalized with photos and mementoes. They were young and old, of several nationalities, some in uniform, some wearing athletic clothes, and one still in pajamas. Lori asked the two questions she had asked so many times already. The blank looks she got foretold the answers before she heard them.

The visit to *Wit's End* was not in vain, however. Anton had counted eighteen bunks, made-up and personalized. And Lori had not seen the member of the crew who Cunningham had said he would *handle*.

4

Anton awoke to the sounds of metal against stone, the rasping of saws, and the calls of men at work. *These are sounds my ancestors awoke to, the sounds of the Azores being built.* Usually, his first thoughts of the day revolved around what Catarina would have for his breakfast. Today, he thought only of getting outside to see how the work was progressing.

The shed was set in a small clearing of a wooded copse at the far end the old dairy, and Catarina had named it *Casa do Bosque*, or House of the Forest. It was being dismantled. Beto shared Anton's sensibilities about preserving the traditions of the Azores. His method was to take apart old buildings, lay in modern plumbing and electricity, and then put everything back in its original place. The exterior was restored to be as it was originally intended, and the interior was finished by craftsmen working in traditional ways to meet the expectations of twenty-first century occupants. Beto had personally overseen the restoration of six old stone houses in this way—houses abandoned when their owners immigrated to America a century before and reclaimed by their descendants in recent years.

Only a few stones remained in place, marking the footprint of what had stood for three hundred years. Anton stared down at the foundation. Ragged stones, probably those cleared from the surrounding field, made a rectangle about thirty square feet. The spaces between them had been filled with pebbles and now-crumbling mortar, mortar just like what one of Beto's assistants was preparing in an old wheelbarrow, grinding limestone to a fine powder before mixing it with water. Anton saw a piece of old mortar with the imprint of a shoe and a small shard of pottery, traces of those who had gone before him, and he was on the verge of climbing over to retrieve them when his wife's voice interrupted his train of thought.

"We have been hard at work while you slept," she teased.

His heart filled with love just looking at her. Catarina had been painting numbers on the stones as they were removed to note where they had been. A scarf covered her hair, and a smear of white paint crossed her chin. She put down her brush to give him his morning hug. They picked their way around the numbered stones and stacks of salvaged wood, and talked about the extraordinary progress Beto and the other men had made in such a short time.

True to form, Anton chatted with each of the workers and even tried his hand at pulling nails and mixing mortar. The pace of activity gradually slowed and the sounds he had awoken to gave way to the sounds of camaraderie, until Beto caught Catarina's eye and she said to her husband, "You are hovering, dear one. Go to the office. Find something to do."

Anton followed his wife's request—at first. He set out for his office, but somewhere along the way, his car took a detour to the airport.

It was rather a grand airport for such a small island. Built by Americans at the end of World War II, it had gradually lost its usefulness as a trans-Atlantic fueling stop, and international flights had been replaced by regional flights. For that, Anton was grateful.

Most flights arrived early, a time of day Anton was not very familiar with, and it was already after eleven by the time he reached the parking lot. When he heard the sound of engines overhead, he quickly squeezed his Volvo wagon into a space meant for a motorcycle and rushed to the tarmac just in time to see a government Cessna touch down long enough to deliver mail to the waiting ground crew. He made good use of both his winning personality and his government identification card to get a seat on its return flight, and twenty-five minutes later he was on São Miguel without paying a Euro.

Anton had been re-thinking Frank Dekker's death. Associating the Americans with it had been a stretch. The note could have been from so many people and meant so many things, and there was no evidence anyone on board *Wit's End* had even been in Santa Maria on the night he died. Catarina's Inspector Morse always said *look to those who were closest to the victim first*. That was why he was in Ponta Delgada, the capital of São Miguel; he wanted to check the land and tax records for Water's Edge. Exactly what he was looking for, he wasn't sure. It would just be more information … but information might be just what he needed.

The available records for Water's Edge and the surrounding land only went back four generations, not unexpected by Anton. What *was* unexpected was how the property was inherited. Contrary to what Anton thought was true under Portuguese law—that a widow would inherit half the estate and the remaining half would be divided among legitimate children—the property had been passed only from father to eldest son. Other than that, he saw nothing remarkable but, as a good detective should, he nonetheless made copies of everything before leaving. *Some detective. That got me nowhere.*

He decided to treat himself to his favorite meal at his favorite café in the historic center of the Ponta Delgada, while he waited for his flight back to Santa Maria. The first thing he did after taking a seat was to call Catarina and tell her he would be home late.

"Where are you now?" she asked.

He grinned. "Just doing some work." The couple was so much in tune with one another that she already knew he was not sitting in his office, and he knew he wasn't fooling her when he used the word *work*.

"So, have you found anything, Detective Cardosa?"

Anton could see her face as she poked fun at him, and he felt some satisfaction in telling her what he had found out. "So, does my investigation compare favorably with what detectives do in England?" He ended with a chuckle.

"Most favorably," she replied, "especially since Detective Cardosa is far more handsome than any detective in England."

"I love you, my darling girl."

"And I love you, my wonderful husband."

They chatted about the progress Beto had made with Casa do Bosque and about their Toni's next football match. Anton heard the admiration in Catarina's voice when she told him what Lori had done. "She has been working on the booklet for the Gillis Foundation representatives. You will love it. Everything you would want them to know is there, and it is so attractive, they will actually *want* to read it."

"I think that should be celebrated!" As Anton grew to manhood, he had kept many of the best qualities of a child: a sense of wonder, seeking and finding joy, dreaming and believing in his dreams—and wanting to celebrate everything from birthdays to sunny days.

Catarina was the more practical one, preferring the security of a larger bank balance. More often than not, however, they went ahead with the celebrations he suggested; she liked to indulge her husband. "What did you have in mind?"

"Let's go to Water's Edge tonight."

He hadn't fooled her. "To Water's Edge, Detective Cardosa!"

The smells from the kitchen were making Anton hungry. While he waited for his order to be taken, he thumbed through copies of what he had found at the records office. The majority were either tax records, all paid on time and in full, or documents formally transferring Water's Edge and the large parcel of land around it from the Costa of one generation to the Costa of the next generation, and from the Dekker of one generation to the Dekker of the next generation. Two liens had been recorded against the property, and both had been stamped as cleared. One secured a bank loan used to expand and modernize Water's Edge; the other was a cash-out transaction dated five months earlier but withdrawn just two days after it was filed.

It was only when the papers were spread out on the table in front of him that he noticed the name of the lawyer representing both Costas and Dekkers had been the same since 1888. That did not strike Anton as particularly unusual, since it was not uncommon for several generations of a family to have men with the same name and the same occupation. What did strike him was that the offices were right there in Ponta Delgada.

Anton was still chewing the hunk of bread that would be his only lunch when he flagged down a taxi at the corner outside the café. He had to make it to the law offices before they closed for lunch and the long rest period that followed. By the time they re-opened, he would be on his way home.

The bronze plaque above the narrow door read *Baretto and Sons*. Although the old building was located near the center of town, the street was already quiet. Many shops had locked their doors, and the tables at nearby restaurants were occupied. He turned a doorknob, polished smooth by at least a century of use, and pushed against the heavy wood door. It was locked. He knocked on the door, waited, and knocked again. Silence. He called out a loud *Hola*. No response. He tried peeking through the shutters on the ground-floor windows with no luck. *What would Catarina think of me now?*

Anton had a very good nose. He was also very hungry. He sniffed deeply, and smelled roasting sausages, toasting bread, and something caramel-y. His very good nose also told him the enticing aromas were coming from inside the building. Perhaps spurred on as much by a desire for food as a desire for information, he made his way down the narrow alley at the side of the building looking for a back door. At the end, he found a small patio where a compact middle-aged man sat enjoying a baguette loaded with chunks of grilled sausage and red peppers. A large white linen napkin, tied around his neck like a bib, protected his neatly pressed shirt. With gray hair and steady brown eyes behind tortoiseshell glasses, he gave the impression of someone you could trust.

Anton watched the bulge in the man's cheeks disappear down his throat and then introduced himself. Here again, his government credentials and a hint that it was a matter of some urgency had the man rising from his chair—alas, without offering Anton any of the feast before him. He headed through a side door, motioning for Anton to follow him as he introduced himself. "I am Miguel Baretto and if this is important, then I am the man to speak to." He led the way to an office that looked as respectable as its owner, outfitted with heavy, dark furniture from the era when heavy, dark furniture connoted prosperity.

Anton began, "I understand you are the lawyer for Francisco Dekker. I wonder if you would answer a few questions about the property owned by him and Mr. Costa."

Baretto was not at all reluctant to talk. This was, after all, not a society where people were preoccupied with possible lawsuits. "Yes. You know we have been the lawyers for several generations of Dekkers and Costas." His face assumed a suitably somber expression. "We heard of Mr. Dekker's death." With that, he left the room.

Anton made himself comfortable in one of the leather wing chairs. In fact, he found himself so comfortable that he pictured one in the Casa do Mar office that he planned at one end of the barn. He checked the time to see if he would be able to have a quick bite of lunch before his plane left, and decided he would—if he got the information he had come for quickly enough.

Ten minutes later, Baretto returned with a cardboard documents box. Anton watched as he took out papers, some old, some new, none organized, and carefully laid them out on his desktop. He kept watching as the lawyer squinted though his glasses, took a handkerchief from his pants pocket, and carefully polished the lenses. Finally satisfied with his glasses, he shifted the papers around until they were in the order he wanted. Anton's stomach rumbled.

At last, Baretto picked up a yellowed piece of thin cardboard that in only fifty or so words gave a description of the property. "This is the first work my great-grandfather did for the Costas and the Dekkers." He passed it to Anton. "The agreement states that the land and everything on that land belongs equally to both men, and each portion can only be inherited in its entirety."

"Could either owner sell his portion to someone else?"

"No. The land is considered a single property, not to be divided." Baretto's response was a relief. Anton's proposal depended on the purchase and conservancy of the entire parcel. "In fact ...," the lawyer continued, "... several months ago, Mr. Dekker tried to borrow against his share." He picked up some papers that had been clipped together. "To finalize the loan, the bank contacted me. They wanted to know of any encumbrances, and I told them that with the terms of the agreement, the property could not be used as collateral without the agreement of both owners."

"With Mr. Dekker's death, where does ownership of the property stand?"

"In terms of the large parcel of land surrounding Water's Edge, it is a simple matter." He picked up another document and handed it to Anton. "This was signed by the grandfathers of Frank Dekker and Matias Costa. At the time, Carlo Dekker had only three girls, and Pedro Costa's first-born son had just died as an infant."

Anton looked at the paper. Baretto pointed to a paragraph and said, "Both men had agreed that only the eldest legitimate son could inherit the property and that this stipulation was to remain in effect in perpetuity."

"What if one of the owners had no son?"

"Then his share would pass to the eldest son of the other owner, but that has never happened in the history of ownership."

"And if neither owner had a son?" Anton was thinking of Frank's brother.

"Spouses and daughters would have a lifetime interest. Then the land would be sold, and the profit would go to the Catholic Church."

"So, right now the property is owned by—"

"—Matias Costa and Paolo Dekker, and the boy's mother will have limited control until he is eighteen."

"Without any provision for Frank's brother, Manuel?"

"Not for the large piece of land, but Water's Edge itself is never to be sold or given to the Church." The slightest of smiles came to his face. "I don't think the idea of the Church owning such an establishment would have been acceptable to the early owners—or to the Church. As far as Manuel Dekker goes, however, I know Matias Costa and Mrs. Dekker, and I am certain that regardless of what happens with the surrounding property, Manuel Dekker will continue to have his place in life at Water's Edge."

Anton raised the issue that mattered most to him. "I have an agreement signed by Matias Costa for the sale of the property adjacent to Water's Edge to the Government of the Azores, and he assured me that Frank Dekker also wanted to go ahead with the sale."

"I do not doubt that Mr. Dekker would have agreed. It is known that he has been trying to sell that property for years—but that is immaterial."

Anton could not breathe.

"Even if Mrs. Dekker, as her son's guardian, wanted the sale, it would be a matter for the court to decide if it could go forward." He took off his glasses and looked at Anton with some degree of regret. "I am sorry to say the court could very well rule that any resolution would have to wait until the boy is eighteen."

The Gillis Foundation grant hinged on acquiring land that might not even be available and without that funding, Anton's appointment had little chance of being extended and Casa do Mar would most likely remain an abandoned dairy. Anton wondered if he had ruined the futures of everyone he held dear.

Anton drove home more slowly than he had ever driven in his life. He needed time to think. *How can I convince anyone to support the conservancy of a piece of land when its purchase may be in doubt for another decade?*

Walking up the driveway, he took in the happiness around him: Liliana making beautiful music on her violin, Toni playing ball with his friends across the road, Catarina and Lori laughing together like old friends. *How precious they are to me.* The sky was reddening and high in the hills around Casa do Mar, soft lights were coming on in the houses of his neighbors. So soon after returning to Santa Maria, Anton already knew them and liked them. That, too, was reason to be happy. He would not accept defeat, he told himself. *I will find a way to save this for all of them.*

Isabella warmly welcomed Anton, Catarina, and Lori to Water's Edge, and Matias and Manuel gave them a tour of the three rooms. The tributes to their shared legacy were everywhere, in the bar top carved with names, in the two chairs—which legend said had belonged to the first Costa and the first Dekker—hanging on a wall, in the row of unopened wine bottles that were supposed to have been bottled before the vineyards succumbed to blight, and in the photographs taken over the past century and a half. They saw large extended families in nineteenth-century dress, the new dining room under construction thirty years earlier, Frank and Isabella as newlyweds, and Paolo as a toddler.

Dinner was the long, relaxed affair everyone on the island agreed it should be. They were seated at a table by a window, where Anton and Catarina shared a comfortable bench with plush pillows, and Lori sank into an armchair upholstered in a Moorish design of coral and gold. The warm glow from the fire on the front patio was reflected in the polished wood paneling and the wineglasses.

Around them, people had settled back for an evening of good food and sociable conversation. It all felt like eating at home on a special occasion.

There was no printed menu; instead, a young woman brought a platter heaped with grilled shrimp and squid, Manuel opened a chilled bottle of a crisp white wine, and they were left to themselves for the next hour. Isabella, who constantly circulated, brought more crusty bread and warm olive oil, and Manuel—who also tended bar in one of the back rooms—returned with a second bottle of wine he wanted them to taste. "This is made in the traditional way, from grapes grown right here on Santa Maria."

Catarina urged Lori to show what she had worked on that day.

"Please make sure he knows this is a mockup, just a concept to show what we will give to the representatives of the Gillis Foundation. It'll look so much better when it's professionally printed on good paper." She opened the cover, still blank, to a two-page map of the island. On it, she had superimposed tiny copies of Catarina's landscapes: rolling green hills in the east, flat chaparral in the west, and a mountainous center with crater lakes and lush forests. Along the coastline, there were a few watercolors of steep black cliffs that dropped to small coves and secluded beaches.

Anton felt a catch in his throat, and it was loud enough to be heard by Lori and Catarina. His wife reached up and hugged his large arm with hers. "Isn't it beautiful?" Her eyes teared when she said, "It makes me even prouder of our people and what we have accomplished." Lori had known since she first heard Catarina's faint Dutch accent that she was not native to the islands; yet, she spoke of the Azorean culture as her own.

Catarina quietly translated the rest, but there was little need. As much as possible, Lori had relied on images rather than text to tell the story of Santa Maria and of Casa do Mar. In the introduction, she pointed to Santa Maria's isolation and lack of development, and made what might have been taken as a drawback into an advantage.

A foldout timeline started 8 million years ago over a rare triple junction of Earth's crust, when Santa Maria emerged through the waters of the Atlantic Ocean, the first land in what was to become the Azores archipelago. It showed volcanoes becoming extinct and seismic activities quieting over time, and the millennia during which fertile volcanic soil accumulated and lush vegetation grew. The island's discovery was represented with old maps, and the history that followed was shown in the ruins of forts built to defend against pirates in the sixteenth century and in the emigrant ships that nearly emptied the island in the nineteenth century.

Other pages showed roads winding between high cliffs, old convents and monasteries, tidal pools rich with marine life, and picturesque villages. One charming page had pictures taken by the mother who was photographing the restoration of Casa do Bosque. Each showed traditional white houses trimmed in the color that reflected what the area around them was known for: blue where woad was once grown to make a dye to replace indigo, yellow where corn and wheat were harvested, red where clay was made into pottery, and green where farms predominated.

Anton was elated.

There were occasional shouts and rounds of raucous laughter from one of the back rooms, but most of the patrons enjoyed relaxed exchanges with friends. Some walked around to talk to visit people at neighboring tables and, naturally, Anton joined them, spotting an acquaintance here, a colleague there.

Catarina and Lori were content to be left alone and watch. "This happens everywhere we go," his wife said. "He is a man who likes to be around people, a man who people like to be around." Standing while others sat, Anton seemed even taller than he usually did, a giant among men, looked to for leadership—and for fun. It had always been that way and, although Anton was almost oblivious to it, it was a source of great pride for Catarina.

Catarina made a short call to check on Liliana and Toni. Especially knowing the extent to which she cared for her children, Lori had been surprised to hear they were to be left alone in the house during dinner, checked on only occasionally by Maria Rosa

Goulart across the road. Listening to the call, she was both happy that she was in a place where it was safe to do that and sad that there were so few such places left on Earth.

In a division of labor that kept everyone busy, Manuel acted as sommelier and bartender, Isabella tended to the other needs of their guests, and Matias travelled to and from the kitchen, delivering the food. About 10 p.m., Matias brought them enormous plates of grass-fed beef, potatoes roasted in olive oil and herbs, and an assortment of young root vegetables. He apologized for the delay. "Estela leaves early to spend time with her children," he explained, "so the later it gets, the busier I get."

Mouth watering, Anton returned to the table and, between bites of dinner, he filled in Catarina and Lori on what he had learned in Ponta Delgada.

Catarina took a small notepad from her handbag. "First, we must ask who might have killed Frank Dekker."

After having heard Catarina chastise her husband for playing detective, Lori was amused to see her doing the very same thing. *She's starting to enjoy this as much as Anton.* Lori understood, though. It was something for both of them to focus on other than what could go wrong with Casa do Mar and the presentation to the Gillis Foundation.

With input from Lori and Anton, Catarina made a list of their suspects.

Isabella Dekker, wife
Manuel Dekker, brother
Matias Costa, partner

They looked at each other. It wasn't a long list. By way of an explanation, Anton shrugged and said, "We are a small community."

Thinking of the British detective shows that were her only addiction, Catarina said, "I have seen many times, the best way to find the murderer is to consider means, motive, and opportunity."

"Means is simple," offered Anton. "Everyone had means; it was just a stone on the beach."

"Were there fingerprints on the stone?" asked Catarina.

"Not a chance. It was rough lava rock, too uneven to have prints." Anton thought back to how the crime scene had been dealt with. *At least no one is responsible for having erased important evidence on the murder weapon.*

"Is it certain that's what was used to …," she let her voice trail off.

"Dr. Leal is certain," he replied. Remembering what he himself had seen, he added, "It was obvious."

"We also need to know who had opportunity," said Catarina.

"When did Dr. Leal say Frank died?" asked Lori. Anton told her it was between nine and eleven the night before his body was found. She had been observing the room. Since they'd arrived, all of their suspects had been in constant motion and had disappeared from view for only short periods of time. "Those are the busiest hours at the restaurant. The chances are that if any of them had gone down to Farewell Beach, it would've been noticed."

"Possibly it was," Catarina reminded her, "but we don't know about it."

Catarina made a note to ask all possible witnesses if they had noticed one of their suspects leaving or returning to Water's Edge the night Frank Dekker was killed. "Now let's look at who might have had a motive."

"None of them seems very upset by Frank's death," Lori contributed.

"Both partners wanted to sell the land but with Frank's death, Matias may not even be able to gain financially," mused Catarina.

"And we have more than what Matias told me to confirm that," added Anton.

"Isabella will probably have some control over Frank's property, but she would have been assured of so much more if Frank had died after the land had sold," Lori said.

"According to the lawyer I spoke with, Manuel gets nothing. He would have never inherited the land and, whatever happened to the property, he would have always had his job."

Catarina summed up the discouraging conclusion, "So, it seems no one will gain financially from Mr. Dekker's—" She stopped short when Matias brought a platter of cheeses for them to sample.

They may not have discussed it in advance, but the novice detectives engaged Matias in friendly conversation—all three of them with the same objective. Cobbling together two languages, they talked first about the weather and the beauty of Santa Maria, then about Anton's plan to secure the heritage of the island. They knew they would be on rocky ground asking about people's whereabouts the night Frank died, so they eased into that slowly, working in tandem so smoothly, Matias remained quite open to talking.

Catarina started. "I am so sorry about Francisco's—Frank's—death."

Matias smiled, a guarded smile that soon disappeared altogether. Lori heard the thinly-veiled ridicule when he said, "Even when we were boys, he wanted to be called Frank. His father tried many times to change that, but Frank liked saying his name should reflect who he was, and he wasn't a man of the islands. He had plans to leave the moment the sale of the land was final." Matias told them the story of the Water's Edge and how the property had been passed down through the generations, exactly as Mr. Baretto had described it. He took pride in his legacy. Then he apologized to Anton for any problem Frank's death might cause. "Even if it was for different reasons, we both wanted to sell the land."

"Did Frank usually work alongside the three of you at night?" Lori asked.

"He was here almost every night." She immediately heard what he had avoided saying. Frank was *here* almost every night, not Frank was *working* almost every night.

"Did you notice his absence?"

"I didn't, but we are very busy at night and ...," he slowed down almost imperceptibly before continuing, "... he was often in the back."

Catarina continued the questioning. "You were here the entire time, yourself?"

"I was. It is my responsibility." Either Matias was very good at controlling his facial expressions or he was truly oblivious to the fact that he was being asked for an alibi—not what one would expect if he were guilty.

"Was Isabella around? Could she have seen Frank leave?"

No one had noticed Manuel come up to the table with a decanter and three small glasses, so he startled them when he said, "It was very busy. Frank wasn't here to help, and there was a large party. Isabella was here every minute. I needed her help until long after midnight to serve drinks and clean up."

Reminded of the evening, Matias was quick to confirm everything Manuel had just said.

Pleasantly sated, they were left alone with their after-dinner liqueurs.

"Well, so much for our investigative skills," said Lori. "Everyone had the means. No one had either the motive or the opportunity."

"It's too early to draw conclusions," cautioned Catarina. "First we must gather evidence. Then we must carefully consider what we have found."

They sat in silence for a while, both Anton and Catarina with the feeling that they had overlooked something significant— but exactly what that was eluded them.

5

Rain had fallen overnight, and Casa do Mar shimmered in the morning light. Each breeze carried air warmer than the one before, and—while Anton slept soundly—Lori and Catarina sat on a low stone wall, enjoying the sunshine. They had long since emptied their second cups of coffee and were watching Beto at work.

The foreman was a tyrant, and they joked about how he must have been a sea captain in a past life. He yelled at masons, waved building plans in the face of the electrician, and dogged two teenage workers, shouting about pipes that had to be brought in and trash that had to be taken away. The building looked further from completion than it had the day before. All of its stones were stacked to one side, trenches to hold new water lines were bordered by mounds of rubble, and ashes from the half-rotted roof timbers that had been burned filled several barrels.

It was before ten when they saw Anton racing towards them in his pajamas. The whirlwind of activity around Casa do Bosque changed his trajectory, and he headed first to Beto, then to each of the workmen, flitting here and there, asking rapid-fire questions, looking around, and moving on. Catarina was waiting when he finally realized that not only was he unable to contribute anything to the restoration, he wasn't even wanted at the job site. She looked pointedly at her watch and said loudly, "Well, the prince has arisen before noon."

It took Anton a moment to remember why he had shot out of bed so early in the day. "I had a dream," he said. "A man on a boat was calling for help."

The two women looked at him dumbfounded. Catarina shook her head. "Is this about Frank Dekker's death? Again?"

Anton gave her a sheepish look. "We forgot about the people on the yacht."

Anton's stature made him identifiable from a distance. By the time he stepped onto the quay, the immigrations official and the customs official were both standing at attention, eyes fixed on him. Lori looked up at her new friend and suppressed a grin. He was lifting his head to the bracing air with an even happier-than-usual look on his face, completely unaware of the deference he was being shown.

Anton was lost in the delightful smells that surrounded him, the smell of brine, the smell of rich earth, the smell of green growing things—the smell of his islands.

Lori cleared her throat and gave him a gentle nudge with her elbow.

He pulled himself away from his reverie, looked at the two men, and said, "I feel sorry for people who do not live their lives by the ocean, don't you?"

The customs official, barely out of his teens, responded, "Ah ... yes ... sir," and waited.

"I called two nights ago about the visitors who came in on that boat." He looked up at the super-yacht that was still docked close by, so white and so large it dominated the marina.

"Yes, sir," the older immigrations man said, anxious to please. "I am José Maria. You spoke to me. I hope the information was useful."

Putting others at ease came naturally to Anton; it was not contrived to manipulate when he put a large hand on José Maria's shoulder, thanked him most sincerely for his help, and struck up a conversation about the importance of his responsibilities in protecting the island.

"Yes," José Maria responded. "We are trained to look for the difference between someone who could bring harm to Santa Maria and someone who is returning." Everyone understood what he meant by *returning*. There were many descendants of the Azorean diaspora around the world, and most of the island's visitors were *returning*—perhaps after an absence of a single generation, perhaps after an absence of many generations.

Anton was not naïve; he was well aware of those who could bring harm to the islands, and of all the ways in which they might do so. It was rare, but swindlers had been known to take advantage of the innocent. Occasionally, tourists on the more populated islands were the victims of petty theft; occasionally, they were the perpetrators. In recent years, young people had been exposed to drugs, usually brought in by foreigners. And a combination of unfamiliarity with roads and alcohol had led to more than a few traffic accidents.

"Did you want me to keep a special eye on the people aboard that ship, sir?"

"Right now, I am just gathering information, but that wouldn't hurt," said Anton. "Do you get many yachts coming into the marina?"

"Mostly they go to Fayal. A good thing, too."

"Do you get many foreigners coming here this time of year?"

"Not really. Sometimes they come for a day or two ... to see the quaint people still living as they did half a century ago, but in the past two weeks I saw only your assistant come in on the ferry," he smiled at Lori, "and only those four Americans come in on their own ship." He thought moment and added, "Of course, I'm not here all the time, but I'll ask others and get back to you."

Miriam Winthrop

Like Anton, he rather enjoyed the thought of participating in an investigation.

"When did it first berth here?"

"The day you called me, sir. Right before the morning ferry from São Miguel."

"You are sure it was not here before that day?" The man's expression was all Anton needed to answer his question. The yacht was far too noticeable to have come into the harbor without seen. "And the people on board, do they spend much time on land?"

"All four went out the morning it docked. My cousin drove them around in his taxi for a couple of hours. He said they were only interested in seeing some coastal land near the new vineyards. I haven't seen any of them leave since."

"So they're all there now?"

"Yes, they are. And I wish I were, too," he replied, completely at ease with Anton.

Anton tried his best to tell Lori what the man had said, and—with his tendency to use gestures and her talent for nonverbal language—she did understand most of it. "You talk Americans?"

Lori confirmed, "You want me to talk to the Americans on the boat?"

"Yes," he said, atypically serious.

"What do I say?"

He patted his left jacket pocket, then his right one, and pulled out a now very crumpled piece of paper.

April 4th
Vila do Porto marina
Wit's End
<u>Both of you</u>.

Lori looked at the paper, took a minute to come up with a strategy, and started walking quickly toward the yacht. For once, Anton was left bringing up the rear. As they drew closer, they heard raised voices coming from the deck above. Captain Sullivan was shouting, "There will be changes on this ship—starting today!"

The same crewman that Cunningham intended to *handle* came down the gangplank and rushed past Lori and Anton, marked with fresh scrapes on his face and a swollen red eye that would soon be black. She put out her hand to stop Anton and guide him into the shadows of some large crates. Then she followed the man to the edge of the dock, where he stood, fuming. She resorted to one of the tools of her trade—her *former* trade—that she had rarely used: she flirted. In her most feminine voice, she opened her eyes wide and breathily asked, "Are you alright?"

In his late twenties, he had a body hardened in the gym rather than by hard labor. In an uninvolved way, Lori could see how some women would find his olive skin and dark features handsome, as she had from a distance. Up close, however, she could see the hair on his head was already thinning and his bright white teeth were somewhat uneven.

"Nothing important hurt." He lit a cigarette and offered her one.

She waved it off and asked, "What happened?" She held her breath, hoping his answer would give her worthwhile information.

"A man's work is sometimes dangerous."

You've got to be kidding.

He seemed to be trying hard to think of something to say. "I was filling in for the Captain, and I tripped over some ropes that were left out on deck."

Right. That's plausible.

"What's a beauty like you doing in a place like this?"

Trying to save it from people like you. Lori giggled and asked him what life was like on the ship.

"No fun and no privacy." He stepped closer. "What's your name?"

"Lori." She could smell stale tobacco on him.

"Jack," he breathed in her face.

Lori tried to bring the conversation around to the people aboard *Wit's End*. She knew their names and faces, but not much more, and she was beginning to feel something like Anton's desperation to figure out who killed Frank Dekker before the Gillis Foundation representatives arrived. She tried not to let anything other than idle curiosity creep into her voice when she said, "Tell me about the passengers on your yacht."

"Why don't I tell you in a more ... personal ... setting?"

Lori forced herself to smile. "Sure. Tonight?" She saw a series of emotions color his face—lust was followed by some recollection, which was then quickly replaced by resentment.

He worked the muscles of his jaw for a few seconds and then said, "I've gotta get the night ferry to São Miguel. I won't be back until Sunday."

Even a child could see he's covering up something—but what? "Oh," she said, feigning disappointment. "Perhaps we could talk about your glamourous yachting lifestyle before you catch the ferry, perhaps you could even show me around."

"No time, sweetheart." He reached out, wrapped a strand of her hair around his finger, and pulled her close.

Behind Hanson, Lori could see Anton approaching with a fierce look on his face, and she wanted to ask one more question before he closed the gap—and possibly gave Jack a second black eye. "Where can I find you when you get back?"

He gave her the name of a small café on a side street near the marina, and she walked away quickly—passing Anton by without a glance and continuing along the dock.

Once aboard *Wit's End*, Anton and Lori went to the pilothouse. Captain Sullivan was there, red-faced and grim. Lori explained that the investigation of Francisco Dekker's death was ongoing, and that Minister Cardosa had a few more questions.

Since she had started questioning people about Frank Dekker's death, Lori had been nagged by the sense that she was getting answers that were honest but intended to lead her astray.

The telltale blinks, the dry mouths, the deep breaths were all giveaways that people were nervous about what she had asked; yet, for the most part, when they answered their voices were steady; they had almost seemed relieved to be able to speak the truth without giving her what she wanted.

Perhaps, she thought, they had been phrasing their responses in a way that would make them true. She decided the solution was to ask the right questions. "I want to follow up on what I asked the last time we spoke," she said, looking Sullivan in the eyes with her most professional Madison Avenue gaze. "First, let me confirm that you did not know Francisco Dekker."

"I did not know a Francisco Dekker."

"He was also known as Frank Dekker."

"I didn't know a Frank Dekker."

Lori wanted to make sure he wasn't just playing a game of words with her. After all, *know* could mean different things. "Did you ever meet someone named Dekker?"

"I did not." His phrasing seemed to indicate that he took her questions as a formal interrogation.

She tried one more time. "He was middle aged, of medium height, a bit heavyset, and he had bright red hair. Are you sure you never saw anyone like that around Wit's End?"

"I am certain." His answer was firm, and his voice was steady. He was pleased to be telling the truth.

Lori dropped that line of inquiry. She held her hand out to Anton, and he gave her the paper that was found on Frank Dekker's body. She looked sideways at Sullivan, but the sight of the paper hadn't elicited any response. "And yet," she said, "this was in the victim's pocket." He read what was written on the paper, and the smile on his face vanished for just a moment before a forced version appeared. Lori knew she had a lead.

Sullivan swallowed hard. "This could have been a meeting with anyone. If it was one of the passengers, it isn't my business. If it was one of the crew, well, then I suppose you could ask them.

"Do you know the crew well?"

"They have all sailed with me before, some many times. I wouldn't have them back if I didn't trust them." The question had made him uncomfortable.

Anton stepped closer to Lori and held up two then three fingers. She understood at once. "How many members of the crew do you have, Captain Sullivan?"

He turned his back on them, and started pressing and swiping the touchscreen on the console. "Eighteen," he mumbled.

"I believe we only saw seventeen when we first questioned the crew. Is the last one on board now?" She knew he wasn't, but she sounded completely innocent.

"Ah, no," he said, still attending to his touchscreen, still avoiding eye contact. "He has limited responsibilities, and tends to come and go a lot."

She knew he was reluctant to give much information and pressed him by directly asking, "His name?"

"Jack Hanson."

"You will let us know when he returns." It was not a question. She gave him her cell number and said—in a way that made it clear it was a demand not a request—she wanted to speak to both Mr. Cunningham and Mr. Stone.

A member of the crew, a young Australian woman, was called to escort them to the main salon, but as soon as they were out of the Captain's earshot, Lori pushed ahead of her. "I can find my way from here. Thanks." She had discovered early in her career just how much could be learned by quietly approaching people who weren't expecting you.

The first voice she made out was Harold Stone's, and he sounded desperate. "We can still move ahead with what we—."

Cunningham interrupted, firm but typically cool, "I know what *you* want. I know what *I* can do."

Stone played the same card he had when Lori eavesdropped on them the day she arrived on Santa Maria. "I only want what is best for our family."

This time, Cunningham showed emotion, and the emotion was anger. "I know what you and Eleanor have been up to, and I have already taken care of *my* family, just as I have taken care of *my* business."

In the silence that followed, Lori knew she had been seen through the window. She pretended to be engrossed in a conversation with Anton, silently mouthing words, and the two had become so in tune with one another, he responded with a look of deep interest on his face. Finally, Anton nodded crisply and took a step ahead.

When they entered the salon, Harold Stone said, "To what do we owe the honor of a second visit, Ms. Moore?"

"The death of Mr. Dekker is of national interest, Mr. Stone. You will understand that Minister Cardosa wants to base any decision he makes on a thorough investigation." Facing both men, she continued without waiting for a response. "You said you did not know Francisco Dekker and had no plans to meet him."

Cunningham spoke first, "As I said the first time you were here, I had no plans to meet this man. I have never been in touch with him." He looked pointedly at Stone, then turned away.

Did he genuinely know nothing, or was he telling Stone to cover for him?

Stone's voice was steady when he echoed what Cunningham had said, "I had no plans to meet Frank Dekker," but his eyes betrayed him.

Under his breath, Anton said to Lori, "Francisco." He was telling her she had never referred to Dekker as *Frank*.

Stone needed information himself. "What makes you think he was coming to Wit's End?"

He had dug an even deeper grave for himself. Lori was cool. "I didn't mean to say Dekker was coming to *Wit's End*." She left it up in the air whether the confusion was because of her wording or his lying.

Anton remained expressionless but he understood. Stone at least knew about the meeting with Frank. The problem was that there wasn't much that could be done based only on a few words that Stone could dispute. In the next moment, however, he truly became *Anton Cardosa, detective.* He made eye contact with Lori and said, "Write."

Lori wrinkled her brow. She didn't understand. She looked into Anton's eyes, hoping for a clue. *Write? Write what?*

Anton saw her confusion. He reached out for the folded magazine scrap, still clutched tightly in her hand. Covering it with one of his hands, he tugged it away from her, all the while looking at her perplexed face. He nodded knowingly at her and secreted the paper in a pants pocket. She shook her head to let Anton know she couldn't figure out what he wanted.

Then it came it her. "Thank you for your time, Mr. Stone. If I could just trouble you for contact information, yours and Mr. Cunningham's, so we can reach you with further questions."

Stone sighed deeply but went to the desk and wrote what she asked for on a piece of *Wit's End* stationary.

Anton and Lori sat in the old Volvo wagon, and stared at what Stone had given them and at the magazine scrap found in Frank Dekker's pocket. There was no doubt; he had written both.

But did he write it at someone else's direction? And who was the other person Stone wanted there when he wrote both of you?

Everything seemed to be going well. Lori had sent files for the Gillis Foundation presentation to the printers, and in record time. There were no feasibility studies, no marketing updates, no meetings with legal, no press conferences to set up. All she had to do was to tell the truth—and it was a truth she sincerely believed in. It had been a pleasure.

Catarina, a talented artist since childhood, had done several sketches to show her vision for Casa do Bosque. It was to be a tranquil retreat, up-to-date yet traditional. She had thought of every detail, from the time-honored motifs of the fabrics to the fragrance of the plants that would fill window boxes on either side of the original oak door. Deliveries from stores all over Europe and America were arriving daily, and the entire family delighted in unpacking them.

Beto had the restoration well in hand. Rubble had been removed, electrical lines were laid in, fixtures for the bathroom had arrived, and stones were being replaced by masons, young men using the same techniques their great-great-grandparents had used.

Catarina and Lori decided to take a couple of hours away from Casa do Mar for a walk along the shore. In that short time, success turned to failure.

Anton was waiting outside the kitchen door when Catarina and Lori returned. He knew his wife had sensed his inner turmoil when the serene face that was so familiar to him changed to one of deep concern.

"What is wrong?" she asked.

Unlike Catarina, Anton usually took no notice of the small worries of life, and generally shook off even the larger ones easily. This time, he couldn't find the words to tell her about them. *Was it all too good to be true? Did I want too much, too fast?*

She moved closer to him. "What happened, my darling?"

He smiled bleakly. "So much has happened." He took a deep breath. "Beto called me at work. He says the drainage pipes for the bathroom are not the right size, and there is no way to have the right ones delivered before the Gillis Foundation visitors arrive."

Catarina wrapped her arms around his waist. "That is just one thing. They will understand."

He hung his head. "There is more. I tried to make reservations from São Miguel to Santa Maria on the 19th, but I forgot there is no service on Sundays. By the time the representatives arrive on Monday, they would only have an hour or two before they have to leave." He sighed. "I'm sorry, darling. I should have thought of these things."

"Your thoughts were on other things, more important things. And remember," she looked up at the face she loved and said firmly, "this is *our* dream, *our* plan, not just yours." She stood on tiptoes and kissed his cheek.

After Catarina translated the bad news for Lori, Anton grimly held out a folder. "Sorry," he said. "Sorry, papers no good."

Lori opened the folder. Inside was what the printers on São Miguel had sent, the presentation booklets she had worked so hard on—or at least some mutant version of them. Overlays had warped, leaving text unreadable, and the colors on pictures had shifted, making skies orange and meadows blue.

Anton apologized again, "Sorry. No time to make good. One week to get special paper to make good."

There was even more, but Anton didn't have the heart to talk about it. As bills for the restoration started coming in, it had dawned on him how much he had underestimated costs. He had spent long hours in his office revising projections, changing plans, downsizing expectations, calculating new budgets, and he had come to the conclusion that there was no way he could make even the small part of his proposal that was Casa do Mar become a reality. For four evenings, he had come home and struggled to put aside his worries, to play with his children as usual, to support his wife in what she was doing. It was the first time in their married life that he had kept something from her.

"This is a difficult time for you, my darling," Catarina said.

"Not that difficult. "Everything will be fine in the end," he replied, but he didn't quite believe his own words.

Lori left the couple alone. She found a seat on a sun-warmed boulder overlooking an impossibly blue ocean and tried to think of ways to help. She had already fallen in love with Santa Maria and Casa do Mar, and with the Cardosas' vision for the future. Most of all, she had already fallen in love with them.

Catarina joined her and for a while, they sat together without speaking. Then Catarina said, "I have never known a time when Anton was discouraged like this."

Lori didn't know what to say and could only manage a sympathetic smile.

"It is because he cares more about others than he does about himself."

"I could say the same about you."

"It is different. Anton takes on the ...," she searched for the right word in English, "... *concerns* of everyone, his family, his village, his entire homeland."

"And he doesn't want to share that burden with those he loves."

An idea formed in Catarina's mind. She nodded slowly to herself, then asked, "Lori, would you help me?"

6

Lori and Catarina had carefully thought through what they were going to say to Anton.

Whether it was a weakness or not was arguable but—since he himself was so honest—Anton rarely recognized deception in others. He was completely unaware that the conversation he heard when he walked into the kitchen the following morning was scripted.

Catarina said to Lori, "I have to go to São Miguel. Some of the things I ordered for Casa do Bosque might not arrive in time." *I'm not lying. They actually might not arrive in time.*

Lori was ready for her part. "I really wanted to see São Miguel before I leave."

"Anton knows São Miguel well." Catarina was choosing her English words carefully and speaking slowly. "He was born there."

The women had agreed Anton would have to be asked for help rather than offered it. "Anton," Lori turned to him, "will you show me São Miguel?"

How could he refuse?

Of course, Anton had made friends with the pilot, Carlos, on their first flight together. He renewed their acquaintance and bought him a coffee while the ground crew unloaded the plane.

Carlos was a young man, tall, trim, and perfectly groomed. He greeted Catarina pleasantly enough, giving her two kisses on the cheek, but it would have been an understatement to say he was captivated by Lori. His eyes locked on her face and, as Felipe had at the police station and as Matias had at Water's Edge, he looked to Anton and then gave Lori three kisses on the cheek—left, right, left.

Following Carlos and Anton to the plane, Lori asked Catarina about it. "Why did you get two kisses, but I got three?"

Catarina chuckled. "A man kisses a woman twice, unless she is unmarried. The third kiss is for luck in finding a husband."

So, as they lifted off for a short, shaky ride over the Atlantic, Lori's mind turned to thoughts she had long since put aside. At twenty-three, when she moved to New York to start her career, she believed that eventually she would meet the right man, marry him, and have children. But the days filled with whirlwinds of activity and the days when nothing much happened had added up to twelve years of her life, and she was left accepting that it was unlikely she would ever live her dream. Looking at Anton and Catarina holding hands across the aisle, though, she found herself thinking about the possibility again.

The trio walked around the *baixa*, or historic center, of Ponta Delgada. Lori found it lovelier than she had thought it would be when she read about how developed São Miguel had become. The beneficiary of trade that grew from lucrative orange orchards in the nineteenth century, the area had attracted wealthy business owners from Europe, in particular Jewish merchants. Anton proudly showed her the ornate banks, old churches and schools, and well-preserved municipal buildings, many ornamented with the same Moorish-style tiles Lori had seen on Santa Maria. Catarina shared the beauty of parks, filled with colorful plants—some of which had become extinct outside the islands—that thrived in a semi-tropical climate brought by the Gulf Stream.

While Catarina and Lori walked around with delighted smiles on their faces, Anton was dealing with mixed feelings. He spent an inordinate amount of time glaring at a tall building that shadowed their steps; although less than twenty stories high, it dominated the landscape—and his thoughts.

Catarina followed her husband's gaze. "Our own skyscraper!" she said. "The view from the top must be spectacular."

"Yes," Anton responded noncommittally, and he began to think. *This is the face of the new Azores.* To his surprise, he realized he was proud of that, too, proud that people had opportunities and advantages they did not have at other times. *Balance. That is the key. We must find a way to have the past and the future.*

Anton hired a taxi driver to take them to a few of the outlying sights. They started in the village of his birth. Twenty years had passed since he last saw it, and much had changed. A hotel, a solid building with a plain façade, stood where his school had been. Where the bakery, the fishmonger, the florist, and his parents' favorite café had been, there was a single supermarket with stacks of brightly-packaged goods in the windows. Most families were now housed in low-lying apartment buildings rather than above their shops or in traditional stone cottages. Only the sidewalks were the same: cobblestones inlaid with white stones to depict the ships, whales, and crosses that were so important in the island's maritime history.

Anton thought about the time he moved away from São Miguel. He was fifteen, for most boys a difficult age to be separated from friends and have to re-establish one's place in a new community. For him, already a strapping six feet in height, handsome and out-going, it would have been trouble-free but for one event.

Both of his parents' families had lived on São Miguel for many generations, his mother growing up on a farm her distant ancestors had started in the 1700s, and his father living above the small general store he had helped run from the time he was twelve. Their marriage had been happy enough—thirty years of peace and moderate good fortune punctuated by occasional struggles but very few heartbreaks. They had had three girls and, later in their lives,

Anton, who shared his name with both his grandfathers. In the three decades the Cardosas had been together, the suburb of Ponta Delgada where they lived had changed greatly, their quiet corner on the only commercial road in the area becoming just one of many corners in a network of new roads that sprawled in all directions. They had found themselves surrounded by other shops, a gas station, three cafés, and the new two-story school. The town was no longer the place his father had pictured when he thought of teaching his grandsons how to fish as he grew old; it was no longer the place his mother had pictured when she thought of teaching her granddaughters how to bake as she grew old.

Still, when an offer was made to buy the general store and home that had housed five generations of Cardosas, Anton's parents had thought very carefully. As is often the case, one small event led to the momentous decision to leave behind all they had ever known. They had been sipping their last cups of coffee for the day and talking over the offer yet again, when a taxi driver honked his horn one too many times, and in a particularly annoying B-flat. They had looked at each other across the kitchen table and nodded, the decision made.

By the end of the school year, Anton's father had—sight unseen—bought a small house on the outskirts of Vila do Porto on the island of Santa Maria, about 70 miles to the south. His reason for choosing that location had been a newspaper article that said of all the islands, Santa Maria was most like it had been before Man first arrived in the archipelago, and his only instruction to the agent had been that the place be in an area with no chance of being developed in his lifetime. In the three months during which Anton finished school, his parents had slowly sold the contents of their family home, finally renting two furnished rooms for themselves, their one unmarried daughter, Kristina, and just six small crates of their possessions. Their plan was to begin a new life that was more like the life they had had as children.

Anton himself was excited. He had always been a boy filled with energy, enjoying risks and discovery, mixing easily with people of all sorts, on the streets and in the schoolyard, in cafés and at church. Approaching the coast of Santa Maria for the first time, his eyes scanned the island, already planning his first adventures.

It was just as the ferry bumped into the dock that he saw the red-haired girl.

Anton, Catarina, and Lori spent a few pleasant hours touring São Miguel. It was not until they returned to Ponta Delgada that Catarina's plan unfolded. Passing the marina, she spoke slowly and clearly to Lori, "I wonder if one of the Americans took that ferry to Santa Maria to kill Frank Dekker."

The scenario was unlikely, she knew. Someone would have had to take the ferry to Santa Maria, kill Frank, and remain hidden until re-boarding *Wit's End* the next morning. But it did start Anton thinking, and she could see that on her husband's face. "What is it, my love?" she asked.

"If someone did take the ferry, they could have gotten back on the yacht by using the swim step Lori and I saw the first time we were on board."

"You think just like Inspector Lewis!" Catarina beamed.

Anton knew he was her favorite detective, and he felt quite proud of himself. "It would only require that his absence not be noticed the night before."

"Or perhaps it was noticed by his wife or someone else, and they choose not to mention it?" she suggested.

"Yes. Yes. Maybe that person is even an accomplice." Anton was warming to the chase.

"Will you check on that?" asked Catarina innocently, knowing that Anton would do exactly as he did.

"Just a short detour," he said, a second or two before telling the driver to drop them off at the marina.

Walking to the ferry company offices, Anton left even the long-legged Lori far behind. "Good morning!" he called out as he swung open the door to an empty waiting room.

A plain woman in her thirties appeared from a back room. "I'm sorry, sir, the afternoon ferries have all left."

Anton pulled out his government identification card, and it elicited the usual response.

"Is there a problem, sir?"

"Not at all. I need to know about the passengers who took the early ferry to Velo do Porto on April 3rd."

She was more than happy to show how competently she managed the office and had gone behind the ticket counter before Anton finished his sentence. Reading from a computer screen, she said crisply, "Records show twenty tickets were sold for that crossing."

"Do you have a list of the names?" he asked. Her smile told him it was a foolish question. People did not have to identify themselves to travel between islands in the Azores. "What about credit card receipts?" he asked, rather proud of his improving investigatory skills.

"Excellent idea, sir. I will cross check my computer records with the paper receipts." A couple of minutes later, she said, "The only charges were for a group of four with the last name of Sousa—returning, probably. The other sixteen tickets were either cash purchases or tickets from a monthly pass book."

Anton sighed. He had not been successful in his detective work. He thanked the woman and returned to Catarina and Lori, who had been watching him through the front windows.

They could see nothing had come of his sleuthing and were prepared to lift his mood with more distractions, but Anton—the man whose mind was always open to other possibilities—found one on his own.

He looked past them to a small, white yacht pulling into its slip and walked away quickly, calling out, "Ask Lori if she remembers the name of the American ship."

"*Wit's End*," said Lori, not needing a translation. Following him, she and Catarina shared more than a smile. In fact, they found it hard to keep their giggles under control. The diversion may not have been unfolding exactly as they had planned, but it was working.

Anton found the immigrations official on duty, showed his identification card, and asked his question.

"I didn't need a name," the man said. "Even in Ponta Delgada, we don't get yachts that large coming in, especially this time of year." He found its arrival in the log easily enough and printed the list of crew and passengers for Anton.

"Is it possible any of them flew to Santa Maria on the 3rd?" asked Anton.

"That's easy enough to check," he replied, checking his monitor, "and the answer is no."

"Did the Americans stay on the boat or on land?"

"How do I know," he shrugged, "but if you could stay on that or in a local hotel, where would you stay?"

An older woman at the customs counter walked over. "I know they got off on the 3rd. They ate at *Ilha Verde*. My children took me there for my birthday that night."

"All of them were at the restaurant?" Anton was close to breathless.

"All? I don't know if it was all, but I do know there were four of them. One of the men insisted on having the largest table by the window, the table we should have had. There were six of us," she complained.

"Did you see what time they left?"

"Americans eat fast. The last ones left long before we did, maybe by eight-thirty."

Anton thanked her. Assuming the four were the Cunninghams and the Stones, which was almost certainly the case, none of them could have taken the ferry to Santa Maria, and none of them could have killed Frank Dekker. At least, he couldn't think of a way it was possible.

He started to walk away, but Catarina stepped up. "Excuse me, *a senhora*," she addressed her deferentially. "You said the last ones left by nine. Does that mean others left even earlier?"

"Yes. They were fighting—and at dinner. Can you imagine?"

Detective Cardosa was back on the case. "Who fought? About what? Who left early?"

"Anton, give the woman a chance," Catarina cautioned. "She is trying hard to remember everything."

The woman smiled at Catarina. "The two men were fighting, but my English isn't good. They disagreed about whether they should do something or not." She stopped and thought back to that night. "The darker man seemed to want it very badly, but the fair man wasn't sure."

"And who left?" Catarina asked gently.

"The fair man."

Cunningham.

"As soon as he was gone, one of the women slammed her hand on the table and started ... well ... scolding the man who stayed. One by one, she held up four fingers, and with each one she seemed to give him an order."

An image of the two sisters came to Anton's mind. So close in age and looks, the one feature that distinguished them was their hair color. That woman was Eleanor Stone.

The customs official was pleased with herself. She, too, watched British detective shows, and she liked to think of herself playing a role in such an important investigation. "And there's something else," she said, "after that, the man made a phone call. The woman listened carefully, and when it was over, both of them were very happy."

"What was the other woman doing all that time?" asked Anton.

"Mostly she ignored them. She looked bored. But it was strange. Everyone, the man who left and the two who stayed, almost seemed to compete over who was taking care of her needs best."

A picture of family life among the Cunninghams and the Stones was beginning to emerge, but what they knew was so limited, it made little sense.

Anton wasn't quite back to his old cheerful self but he was, at least, preoccupied with something else. With the list of the passengers and crew of *Wit's End* in hand, he headed to his next stop, almost unaware that the two women who had arranged the entire adventure were trailing behind him.

Police headquarters was in one of the historic buildings in the baixa. After showing his credentials, the three of them were shown into the office of Pedro Medina, chief of the Judicial Police. Tall and strongly built, he would have been an attractive man if not for an extremely long and red nose. He offered them seats and spent a few minutes talking to both Catarina and Lori about their impressions of Ponta Delgada. His English was very good.

Switching languages, Anton cut in. "I want to ask about some Americans who came into the marina on—," but he was quickly cut off.

"Why is this of interest to a Minister of Culture?" he challenged Anton. The man was not going to allow an amateur to step into what might be police business.

Anton hesitated. He was a gentle man, more comfortable with cooperation than with confrontation.

Lori, on the other hand, was quite familiar both with men like Pedro Medina and with how to deal with them. She stepped forward and twisted the truth. "Let me apologize. The central government office .... The Presidente is part of the central government, right?" she asked with wide-eyed innocence.

Anton and Catarina stared at her, dumbfounded.

"Anyway, Minister Cardosa is trying to help me." *He is trying to help many people.* "I am thinking about writing an article about effective ways to deal with crime. *I'm thinking about doing many things.* "It is sometimes best to describe complex situations by profiling how a single individual deals with them." *This could be your chance at fifteen minutes of fame, Pedro. Or not.*

She saw him straighten his spine and lift his chest, sure signs that he was now trying to impress her. "Would you be willing to talk for a few minutes, and would you have an official photo I could have?"

"Yes. Yes," he replied eagerly.

Lori spent a few minutes talking to him about local crime, which had gone from essentially non-existent twenty years before to barely worth noting. "We have had a small," he emphasized just how small by bringing a thumb and forefinger close together, "problem with drugs among the young people in the past few years, so small that finding any evidence of it is a problem." He turned to Anton and said, "That is to be expected with so many outsiders coming to São Miguel."

Lori seized on that comment to get closer to what she wanted to know. "I'm sure you do as good a job as possible keeping an eye on who enters the island."

"Yes. Yes. We check the names of people who enter against an Interpol database."

"So, I could just show you names ...," she pretended to be trying to think of an example, then snapped her fingers and asked for the list of people on *Wit's End* that Anton had been given, "... like this, for example, and you would actually be able to look at it and know if one of them had a background you should be interested in?"

He looked at the list. He didn't say a word, but he didn't have to. The smile remained on his face until he reached the very bottom of the list, where the name Jack Hanson was. His demeanor changed. He stiffened and drew his lips together. He knew he had been flattered into talking, and he was angry. His responses became guarded, they were told he was out of time, and they were shown to the door.

With no legitimate status to investigate any crime, not to mention having lied to the Chief of the Judicial Police, Anton decided not to protest.

Before they even reached the sidewalk, Lori reminded him that Jack Hanson appeared to have been hiding something when he talked with the teens by the fuels tanks. Anton set his jaw and walked purposefully ahead of her. She wasn't prepared for the reaction she saw when she caught up with him.

The perpetually mild-mannered man turned, punched the air with a fist, and said grimly, "Not on my island."

7

To thank Lori for all she had done, Catarina invited her to lunch— at Water's Edge.

"Alright, Catarina, confess."

Catarina was puzzled. "Confess?" Her first thought was that she had done something her guest did not like.

"Why are we here at Water's Edge and not some other restaurant?"

"Well, there are very few ...," she started with an excuse but quickly laughed at herself. "I had not thought of it when I decided to ask you for lunch but, yes, we are here because I have become as intrigued by the mysterious death of Francisco Dekker as my husband is."

They positioned themselves at their table so they could observe Matias, Isabella, and Manuel. They would take advantage of Lori's gift for reading interactions between people and of Catarina's gift for understanding people's feelings, even when they hid them from themselves.

Estela, the waitress who left early every night, was a pretty, petite young woman with bouncing dark curls and friendly brown eyes. She gave them a choice of soup or roast chicken, and left them to enjoy their bread and the view of a particularly blue ocean.

"She might be someone to ask questions of," said Lori.

"Precisely, a *disinterested party*, as Chief Inspector Barnaby would say."

"You're becoming quite a detective yourself," Lori laughed.

"Anton is the good detective."

"And, of course, you're not showing any favoritism," Lori teased her.

Catarina thought for a moment and said, "The truth is that each of us is one facet of a good detective, and collectively the three of us make one complete good detective. Rather like a detective trinity," she chuckled.

"The Trinity Detectives," Lori declared somewhat grandly.

Manuel came over to their table with a bottle of wine. He looked like a man worn down by life, his face almost expressionless and his voice a monotone. *"Boa tarde, as senhoras,"* he greeted them formally in Portuguese. "Would you like a glass of wine before the food comes?" He didn't actually wait for a reply before pouring.

Catarina engaged him in conversation and carefully observed his demeanor. When Lori had told her there wasn't a trace of sadness on Manuel's face when he heard of his brother's death, Catarina hadn't found that significant. She knew that grief can manifest itself in many ways. Offering her condolences to Manuel, however, she noticed something else; Manuel didn't even seem to even acknowledge a personal connection to Frank Dekker.

Sipping her wine, this time a cold and fruity one, Lori watched Matias, who was lost in thought, dusting the pictures that captured the history of Water's Edge. It took her a few moments to figure out how what she saw was different from the first time they had eaten at the restaurant: there was a telltale rectangle of brighter paint, the space where a picture had recently been, the picture of Frank and Isabella at their wedding.

Estela brought them deep bowls of a seafood soup that would have put the best cioppino to shame. Filled with fresh mussels, shrimp, and scallops, it was the essence of the ocean itself. "I'll bring you more bread," she said. Lori almost said no, but she knew that—short of licking the bowl—she would need it to get every possible drop of broth into her mouth.

Catarina decided it was time to talk to her *disinterested party.* After checking to make sure no one else was within earshot, she asked in English, "Have you worked at Water's Edge long?"

"About ten years now, since I was seventeen."

"The death of one of the owners is terrible."

Estela's response was a mumbled *mmm*.

"How is everyone doing?" asked Lori, lifting her eyebrows to Matias, who was now dusting the memorabilia on shelves around the room. "He seems preoccupied."

"Matias? He's always that way. He loves this place. When I first came, he showed me every wood carving and piece of scrimshaw in there …," she pointed to the painted wood figures and the engraved whales' teeth in a small glass-fronted cabinet, "… and he told me a story for each one. He's very proud to carry on the traditions of his ancestors."

Lori could understand why Matias supported Anton's plan for Santa Maria. "Did Frank feel the same way?" she asked slowly in English.

"Frank?" Estela suppressed a smirk. She answered in Portuguese and far too quickly for Lori to follow.

After she left, Catarina translated, "Apparently, from the day he received his inheritance, Frank was determined to sell the surrounding land and leave Santa Maria."

"That wouldn't have affected Water's Edge, though."

"True. This place would still be legally owned by a Costa and a Dekker, and run by the same people."

Lori began to rehash what they had talked about the last time they sat in Water's Edge. "That means life would continue as it is for Matias, whether Frank was alive or dead."

Catarina nodded slowly but said nothing.

"In fact, I don't see how life would change for any of them. According to the lawyer Anton talked to, Manuel would still have his position and his home here. Isabella might—just might—have some control over a portion of Paolo's inheritance, but that's quite a longshot to commit murder. Most likely, the land can't even be sold until Paolo is eighteen, and he would get the money not her."

Catarina was barely listening. Just like the last time they ate at Water's Edge, she had the nagging feeling she was forgetting something, but every time she tried to pin down her thought, it escaped her.

Lori kept sorting through facts. "If Frank were alive and wanted to divorce his wife, why would she kill him before the land was sold? And why was she so calm when Anton told her about Frank's death? I swear I even saw a small smile on her face at one point."

Catarina peeled a shrimp, lost in thought. She knew she was overlooking something important.

Matias came over to refresh their wine glasses. "Do you like it?"

"Yes. *Sim. Delicioso.*" Lori's took the opportunity to practice the little Portuguese she had learned so far. "*Bordo do Mar*," she used the Portuguese term for Water's Edge, "is special. I hope you do not change it." After what Estela had said, she knew she was hitting a nerve.

Matias stiffened. "Change? There are no plans to change Water's Edge."

"I'm so glad. I thought I heard Mr. Dekker had plans to change something," she lied.

"Frank always had big plans," he said bitterly, "but not for this place. The Earth could have opened up and swallowed it, and it would have meant nothing to him—as long as he could sell the land and run away from what our ancestors gave us."

This is not simple indifference. This is hatred.

At the end of the meal, Lori and Catarina talked over what they had learned over their espressos. Each came to the same conclusion: they were further from finding out who had killed Frank Dekker than they had been before lunch.

"Perhaps Anton is right. Perhaps one of the Americans on the yacht killed him," Lori said.

"I can't imagine a motive for any of them, either." Catarina replied thoughtfully. "Besides, none of them had the opportunity."

Both women sighed.

Catarina hesitated a moment as they went down the steps to the sidewalk. Then she linked arms with Lori. "Thank you," she said ever so quietly, *"minha amiga."*

Lori understood. Catarina had not used the words lightly when she called Lori her friend.

The nature of Catarina's childhood had left her acutely aware of the dynamics of social groups, and wary of making her way into ones that were already established when she came into the picture. With Lori, she felt the possibility of a friendship with a depth she had not experienced in many years.

Sixteen-year-old Catarina first saw Santa Maria from the air. As the plane circled the island, her father pointed out the circular dish of the European Space Agency satellite tracking station, where he would be working. Petrus Vanderhye was a communications engineer, working in a field that—in the early 1980s—was growing beyond all imagining. Cables were giving way to optical fibers, and satellites were making the need for any physical connection obsolete.

Little would change for her—or so she thought. It was another house, another school, another country, as her father followed the demand for the new technology around the world. She would still have to make new friends—not easy for a shy child—and then to say goodbye to them just as she began to feel comfortable and have fun. She would still be on the periphery of a different culture, looking in and not really belonging. She would still not be able to have the dog she had always yearned for.

Several years before, her parents had given her an ongoing assignment to keep a record of the thousands of miles she had travelled, with essays on what she had learned in each new place. They said the same thing each time they told her to update her journal. *Aren't you a fortunate child, Catarina, to have travelled so widely?* The first thing she did when she moved into her room at college was to put the journal in the trashcan.

Lisolotte Vanderhye was a nurse, a profession in demand wherever in the world the family moved. When she arrived on Santa Maria, Dr. Leal's young nurse, who was also his bride, had just died, and Catarina's mother kept herself busy working at the doctor's clinic four days a week. The only interactions the Vanderhyes had with their daughter were brief, somewhat impersonal, and centered on their expectations for her accomplishments.

Catarina, always a serious child, was left to herself even more than usual during the months of summer vacation before starting school on Santa Maria. Most days, she took one of the walking trails that threaded the island, carrying lunch and a book. She was always reading. Sometimes she tucked a pencil into her pocket to make notes in the margins of her book, something her parents looked on with such contempt that it was likened to a sin. For Catarina, however, writing felt a bit like having a conversation with the author or other readers, and she felt less alone.

Catarina liked Santa Maria. Sometimes she sketched what she saw on the blank end pages of a book, and she still had those old sketches of coastline villages, wildflowers, and grazing cows. She especially liked the stone houses. Their permanence appealed to her; some had stood for four hundred years and would probably be there hundreds more. She made detailed drawings of an embellishment she found on many of the houses: distinctive chimneys. Cones, trapezoids, or pyramids, they resembled Moorish minarets and were a legacy of the first settlers from the Algarve region of Portugal. When she and Anton moved into their first home, she had six of those pages framed, and they still hung on their bedroom wall, a record of her early days on Santa Maria.

That same summer, Anton's family settled into its new life on Santa Maria. He made friends and started to explore the island. With a knack for turning a hike or a swim into an adventure, he soon became the daring leader of a group of teenage boys who found rock walls to climb, offshore craters to fish in, and dark caves to explore. He even made their late-afternoon walks through town or around the marina into exciting activities, filled with daydreams of travel and fearless escapades. He was not to make the connection until almost thirty years later, but the one exploit that was always just beyond their reach was drinking at the rough-and-ready bar the men spoke of as *Our Place:* Water's Edge.

He had not forgotten the beautiful red-haired girl he had seen as the ferry pulled up to the dock in Vila do Porto. Exactly what fascinated him, he would never be able to explain, even to himself, for it was just a glance, and he had yet to discover all the wonderful qualities he would find in his first love. Everywhere Anton went, he looked for her. When he wandered through the maze of streets around a village square and heard the sound of a voice that might be hers, he pulled his face into what he thought would be a more attractive pose and ran fingers through his unruly hair. When, at the end of a strenuous activity, he rested with his friends on one of the rocky outcrops that pebbled the island, he scanned nearby walking trails looking for a flash of red hair. He even went to church a couple of times, sitting at the back and looking out over the congregation for her. At night, he fell asleep to plans for what he would say to her when they did meet and how they would spend their lives together, for he was certain they would. And that certainty didn't seem odd to Anton at all.

One month after his family moved to Santa Maria, Anton's mother went into the hospital on São Miguel. She would never return home. Almost overnight, his family disappeared. Travelling between the two islands was expensive and lengthy, so his father reluctantly returned to his home village and lived with relatives. When Anton got up in the morning, his sister had already left the house for her job at a grocery store, where she met the man she would marry the week before her mother died. When Anton returned from school in the afternoon, his sister was either out with her new boyfriend or closeted in her bedroom, talking to him on the phone. No dinner waited for him. No one asked him how his day had been.

After his mother's funeral on São Miguel, Anton went back to his new home on Santa Maria, hoping to return to a life more like the one he had enjoyed before his mother became ill. That was not to be. Days later, his father died suddenly and Anton—the boy who loved people—was left essentially without a family.

Anton's charm and good manners had always made him a favorite of his teachers, but he was not a good student. He saw little purpose to academic work and had every intention of following in the footsteps of so many young people on the island and immigrating to America, where—so the word was among his peers—a good life could be had without any advanced degree. That first summer on Santa Maria, he looked forward to the start of school for the usual opportunities to socialize—and to finally meet his red-haired girl.

Catarina was not at Anton's school. Her parents had determined that it was best for her to attend a small school set up by the wife of one of the American officers at the nearby military base. There were only two classes, one for younger children and the other for those older than twelve. The children were taught in English, a language the Vanderhyes considered essential, and lessons focused on the academics necessary for admission to university. Catarina found herself in a group of six girls and boys, every one of them four years younger than she was.

She had learned to embrace her solitude, and she immersed herself in her studies, something that pleased her parents enough to leave her alone on that account. She looked ahead to her college years and to finding a likeminded man, a professor perhaps, so she could raise a family of her own. And she imagined watching her children grow in the same house, and planting a flower garden, and having a dog.

Catarina's parents noticed she had a talent for drawing, so they arranged for a taxi to take her to private art lessons after school twice a week. Even more than the idea of learning something new, she liked the idea of walking back home by herself. At that hour, houses would be lit for the evening and she would be able to see through the windows to the families gathered inside.

When she walked into the art studio at the local school for her first lesson, the teacher was scolding a student. It was the gentlest of scoldings, delivered with an indulgent smile. "What am I to do with you? You had no essay for the third week in a row."

There was no response; in fact, the student wasn't even looking at the teacher, not because he was shamed but because he had turned his head when the door opened and there, standing right beside him, was his red-haired girl. As soon as he recovered his voice, he said, "I'm Anton. You're new here, and I'll help you whenever you need something." He managed a crooked smile.

Catarina looked up at the tallest, most handsome boy she had ever seen. "Thank you," she said quietly, and Anton's heart soared. She addressed the teacher, "I am Catarina Vanderhye, and I am here for art lessons."

Anton broke his gaze and turned to the teacher "Professora, I am sorry, so sorry that I will stay right now and do the essay before I leave." For the next hour, Anton watched his red-haired girl's hands move as she turned a lump of clay into a dog and, when the art lesson was over, he suddenly got up, slapped the essay he had been distractedly writing on the teacher's desk, and left.

The day he finally met his true love, Anton followed her home—as he would on many other days—for the simple pleasure of watching her move. He rediscovered the limber, lean body he had seen climbing out of a rowboat on the day he arrived on Santa Maria. He marveled at the length of her arms and legs, the rosy whiteness of her skin, the gleam of her red hair. He smiled at the way her hips swayed, how her sweater pulled one way and then the other, how the books she carried pressed against her side.

Even then, Anton was a man of vision, and even then, he had the determination to make his vision reality. He arranged to make up each week's late work at the same time and in the same place as Catarina's art lessons. He saw determination in the way she perfected a sketch or improved the shapes she modeled from clay. He heard her intelligence when she and the teacher talked about artists and history and books he had not known existed. He admired how confidence and shyness both retained their own qualities in her one person, and how she carried herself with quiet dignity. As fall turned to winter, he fell in love with her, and he sensed that sharing a life with her would make him a better person, and would make her a happier person.

It was December before he made his first move. He had already learned where she lived, when she returned from school each day, and when she was alone in the house. He dressed carefully, bought a small bag of cookies at the bakery, and caught up with her just as she reached her front door. He asked if she would like to accompany him to the *arraial*, a village fair with folk music and traditional dances.

By that time, Catarina had become aware of the boy who seemed to cross her path so much more than anyone else on the island. She was surprised by how comfortable she felt around him; in fact, she looked forward to seeing him in art class every week. She was glad Professora was so lenient and allowed them talk while she drew. Anton helped her with her Portuguese, and she relied on him—perhaps more than she had to—because she saw how it made him feel good.

The arraial began late, after the usual dinner hour; even if the invitation were not from an unknown local boy, Catarina knew that fact alone meant her parents would not allow her to go. For the first of what would be many times, she said goodnight to them, turned off her bedroom lights, and climbed out the window, knowing they would never check on their obedient daughter.

Sometimes Anton planned bike trips and hikes for them, times when they could be alone, and sometimes they joined his group of friends at cafés or at the beach. It was obvious to Catarina that everyone adored Anton, and it was exciting to be courted by the most popular boy on the island. Thanks to Anton, she enjoyed a social standing among other young people that she had never had. Thanks to Anton, she was connected to a place and a people.

By spring, she thought of him all the time. *What is he doing right now? What will he be wearing tomorrow? Who was he talking to before I walked in?* As much as Catarina believed Anton felt deeply for her, however, she didn't allow herself to fall completely in love. She was keenly aware of how relationships could be suddenly ended by a new school, the end of a job assignment, an unexpected move.

Then one day, her bike broke on the way to meet Anton at their favorite spot near an old dairy. She knew she would never make it in time. True, she was disappointed not to be able to see him, but there was more. She felt an empty space beside her, a place where he should have been, and she started to imagine life without him. The terrible desolation she felt led to the realization that if she felt that way, surely she must be in love.

The chance event of seeing a red-haired girl climbing into a rowboat had changed so much about two lives.

8

Anton, Catarina, and Lori had reached the same conclusion: the preservation of the land around Casa do Mar was their joint mission, and it would not fail because they gave up. Over breakfast—for which Anton appeared at the unheard of time of 8 a.m.—they talked over each of the obstacles they faced and any solutions that might help.

Lori had faced challenges such as the fiasco with the booklets before. That would not stop her from doing the job she had been hired to do. "I'm going back to Ponta Delgada this morning. I'll be back late, and I'll have the materials, and they *will* be perfect."

Catarina was going to spend the day looking into every possible way to give the representatives of the Gillis Foundation more than a couple of hours on Santa Maria. She had already started a list of private plane owners on all the islands, and she planned to use her husband's name freely when she tried to find a government plane that might be able to fly their visitors across the strait before Monday morning.

Anton would make sure that—missing drainage pipes or not—the restoration of Casa do Bosque was completed on time. For him, the most difficult time came after he dropped Lori off at the airport. He told Catarina that their savings were depleted, and Casa do Mar would be limited to the one new guest house for a very long time—perhaps forever if it did not generate enough income.

"We have always made it, dear one, haven't we?" Catarina said.

He acknowledged her with a small nod, signifying only that he had heard her.

"We are not relying on Casa do Mar alone. You are a Minister of the Azores," she said with pride.

"Perhaps just for the next year," he countered, but weakly enough that his wife knew he still had hope for the future.

"So much can happen in a year, my love. We will have a year in paradise with our children, a year to set Santa Maria on a course that will honor its heritage forever."

"*If* we get the grant from the Gillis Foundation." He was not being pessimistic; he was proclaiming his commitment to make that happen. He hugged her close. "I'm sorry, my red-haired girl."

"There is nothing to be sorry—"

He cut her off. "I know this is hard for you. I know *why* this is hard for you."

She reached up and laid her hand gently on his cheek. She knew he didn't want her to be faced with feeling rootless, as she had been in childhood. True, there might be another house, another community, another country even ... but it would not be as hard for her as Anton worried. Catarina now carried her roots—her family—with her.

Lori caught the morning mail plane. Looking down at the tiny island of Santa Maria, surrounded by a vast and fierce Atlantic, she felt something like Anton's determination to save it.

Laptop and portable drive in hand, she went to three printers in Ponta Delgada, eliminating one when no one there spoke English and another when no one understood the technical requirements of the job. At the third, she offered a bonus—out of her own pocket—as well as a testimonial she would post for them, if they could work together until the job was done right. It took four hours and countless versions, but the result was just what she had intended. The booklets reflected both competence and passion, and clearly laid out the proposal's importance in preserving a special culture.

Lori leaned over the ferry railing, her teeth chattering in the cold wind. From above, the ocean was inky black, but where swells rose and sunlight travelled through them, they were jewels of purest aqua. It took a moment for her to realize that the dark spots in the waves were dolphins, and she closed her eyes to make another memory.

The ferry entered the Velo do Porto harbor earlier than expected. She was taking out her phone to ask Anton if he could pick her up, when she spotted Jack Hanson standing in a dimly-lit spot behind stacks of crates on the dock, hidden from the view of everyone in the marina. It was quite clear what he was doing there.

She turned on the video camera and recorded Hanson as he gave small packets to three teens in exchange for cash. The transaction didn't take longer than thirty seconds but, along with testimony from the kids, the video might be the hard evidence Chief Medina had said the Judicial Police needed.

Lori was about to turn off the camera when she saw Carolyn Cunningham peering around a tall crate. The rest happened so quickly, she didn't know where to point her camera first. Carolyn Cunningham started toward Hanson, her husband came up behind her and pushed her aside, and the two men lunged at each other. They struggled and, off-guard, Matthew Cunningham tilted precariously over the edge of the dock before finding a handhold on a lamppost. His wife ran to Hanson and, as the ferry came closer and closer, Lori could hear the sound of Matthew Cunningham's voice, yelling as he made his way back to the pair. He had attracted the attention of other passengers, who themselves yelled and even laughed at the three Americans. Hanson and

Cunningham looked up and made eye contact with Lori, who still stood pointing her camera at the scene.

As the ferry thudded into the dock, the men started grappling. They were well matched, and each time Hanson tried to escape, Cunningham pulled him back. Finally, Hanson flung an outstretched arm out in the direction of Carolyn Cunningham, who was knocked over the edge of the dock, landing hard in a moored rowboat. At that Hanson fled, and Cunningham climbed down to his wife's motionless body.

Lori was breathless when she called Catarina. "Please ask Anton to come to the marina right away. And call for an ambulance and the police. Something has happened."

Santa Maria's entire police force had been summoned to the marina. Lori handed her cell phone over to Anton and, through Catarina, explained what she had seen. Felipe stood at attention, waiting for direction and somewhat pleased to have an important police task ahead of him.

Without a word, Anton led the way toward *Wit's End*, each long stride matched by two from the men who followed. At the foot of the gangplank, he realized he had no good way to question the Americans on board, so he urgently waved Lori forward to join him. He was not going to let any time pass, time in which Hanson could cover his tracks. *I will have him off my island.*

By the time they reached the main deck, the crew had been alerted and was gathering. Standing just a few inches from Captain Sullivan, Anton's stature alone would have been intimidating but when he spoke, his voice was thunderous enough to make everyone blink.

Lori could not match his anger when she addressed the Captain, but her voice was hard. "Minister Cardosa asks how well you know the crew you are responsible for, and whether you really *know everything that happens on this ship.*" She had chosen her words and intonation to match what Sullivan had once said: *I know everything that happens on this ship.*

He opened his mouth, then shut it quickly. Even the fearsome Captain was silenced. He glanced left and right at the crew standing around him and, trying to give the impression that he was still in control, he said, "Let's talk in the sky lounge." He turned and walked away, leaving the entire crew wide-eyed.

Lori, Anton, and the four policemen followed him inside. None of them accepted his offer to take a seat. Lori followed up the questions she had asked on deck with a simple and pointed, "Well?"

The Captain made an effort to regain his composure. "What is it you want to know?"

"You can start by telling us about Jack Hanson."

"He is a crew member who sailed from Newport with us. I don't know much about him."

Lori heard the dryness in his mouth. He was lying. She looked at Anton, and he boomed an order to his men. They immediately surrounded Sullivan, and Felipe unsnapped a pair of handcuffs from his belt, apparently the only pair among the four policemen, and a very old pair at that.

Sullivan put his hands up in mock surrender, "Alright. Alright. What is it they want?"

Lori gambled. "We know you are aware of Hanson's activities."

Again the Captain opened his mouth to speak but thought the better of it and remained silent.

"This is your chance—your only chance—to speak up, unless you want a criminal record, too."

He spoke slowly and carefully, considering each word, "It came to my attention that Hanson might be selling drugs—," he corrected himself and said firmly, "—*was* selling drugs."

"What did you do about that?"

He drew himself up and tried to salvage his dignity. "I thought the best course of action would be to deal with him myself."

He was still covering the truth. "Why was that the best course of action? Why not tell the police? Why not kick him off the boat?" Suddenly, Lori knew why not. "Where is your daughter, Captain?"

He reached out to the piano. The shiny ebony reflected the trembling in his hand before he pressed it down to steady himself. "My daughter? What does my daughter have to do with this?" He looked like any loving father might when faced with hurting his own child.

Lori felt sorry for him, but it was time to play hardball. She turned to Anton, made eye contact, and spoke very clearly, "Minister, with your permission, could the Chief get Captain Sullivan's daughter and bring her here?"

Anton picked up on her slight nod. She wanted him to agree to something, but he wasn't certain what. He said, "Yes," in English and looked at Felipe, hoping he had understood what Lori said. "Felipe!"

It wasn't necessary for Felipe to understand anything. Lori had called the Captain's bluff. He sadly agreed to bring his daughter to the sky lounge. When he returned ten minutes later, his arm was wrapped protectively around the tiny young woman. She looked better than she had when they last saw her, less dazed and pinker in the skin, but still frail.

"This is my daughter, Kimberly. She has been … sick …." He set his lips and started again, "She … Hanson … introduced her to …," he couldn't even bring himself to say the word.

Kimberly leaned against her father. "It's alright, Daddy. I can tell them." He held her even closer while she spoke. "Jack didn't introduce me to anything. What can I say? Drugs are everywhere. This started a long time ago."

The Captain swallowed hard.

She turned to him, "I'm sorry, Daddy. Really."

He set his lips and nodded at her.

"Daddy brought me with him to keep me away from the pills, but Jack was … well … Jack caught on to my …."

"He sold you what you wanted?" asked Lori.

"No," she snickered when she explained what Hanson had done. "He *gave* me what I wanted, gave it to me, so—"

"So I would cover for him!" Sullivan spat out. "So wherever we went, he could do what he does—spread his filth!" He took a deep breath, but shame kept him from saying more.

"And where is he now?" asked Lori.

"He knows I'm keeping Kimberly away from him. He doesn't have anything to hold over me. I made that clear."

"Was that when we were last aboard? Hanson had just been roughed up."

Sullivan set his jaw. There was no contrition in his voice when he said, "Yes. I did that. He deserved more. He won't come back here. You're welcome to search stem to stern."

"We will." Lori felt her heart racing. *We did it. We actually got to the truth.* She decided she had covered everything and was preparing to leave, when Anton nudged her.

"Frank," he said meaningfully, his eyebrows disappearing into his shaggy brown hair.

She remembered how Sullivan had blinked when he said he didn't know Frank Dekker. This time she looked into his eyes like someone who had already caught him in a lie, and she allowed him no wiggle room. "One more thing, Captain Sullivan. Tell me *everything* you know about Frank Dekker."

"Dekker," he exhaled deeply. "Look, the private business of my boss, of Mr. Cunningham, is … well, private."

Lori knew he was going to talk anyway, so she said absolutely nothing.

"All I know is that Stone told me Mr. Cunningham would have a guest by the name of Dekker join us on our return to São Miguel. Then, late on the day we docked, Stone said it was all a mistake and Dekker wouldn't be coming."

She couldn't resist saying, "It would have been better for everyone if you hadn't withheld that information—twice." Lori turned and, accompanied by Anton and the Santa Maria police department, walked out. Along the way, she couldn't resist nudging Anton. They made eye contact and exchanged broad grins, both thinking the same thought. *True detectives at last!*

Lori asked a passing crewman to direct them to the Cunninghams' private quarters. There she found Carolyn Cunningham, barely occupying a quarter of an enormous bed, and Maria Rosa Goulart, the Cardosas' nearest neighbor, unwrapping a blood pressure cuff. A heavyset young woman with blond hair pulled into a knot at the back and a stethoscope draped around her neck, the first impression she gave was of seriousness and competence. The other side of her, the side that emerged when she was stirred up by drama, appeared as soon as she looked up.

Maria Rosa immediately launched into a nonstop monolog, talking so quickly in Portuguese that Lori, who was beginning to pride herself in how much of the language she had already learned, was not able to understand a single word.

Poor Anton found himself backing against a wall as Maria Rosa filled him in on the condition of her two patients, asked about what had happened, speculated on the whereabouts of the escaped criminal, and deplored the lack of safety on the island—all without seeming to take a breath.

More than once, Lori saw Anton try to wedge in a few words of his own, but he couldn't seem to bring himself to simply interrupt and put an end to Maria Rosa's speech. So she did. "Anton," she almost yelled. "How are the Cunninghams?"

Anton gratefully squeezed around Maria Rosa. He looked to Lori ask that very question, "They are good?"

She addressed Matthew Cunningham, "How are you and your wife doing?"

Predictably, the man was composed. "I am well, myself, just a few minor scrapes. My wife took a bad fall. If this—What is she, a doctor? a nurse?—would calm down, I might know more about how she is."

Lori faced Maria Rosa, extended her hand, and said slowly in English, "Catarina, Anton's wife, introduced us a few days ago," she reminded her. "I am Lori. I am staying at Casa do Mar."

Having to talk in an unfamiliar language slowed her down. "Yes. I am ...," she could not come up with the correct term in English, "... like doctor."

"I remember. You are what we call a nurse practitioner. How is Mrs. Cunningham?"

"Yes." She inhaled deeply and tried to assume a more professional tone. "I look at the patients. The patients good. The patients must sleep. I will come tomorrow."

Lori looked at the Cunninghams, both bandaged and marked with welts. She was asleep, and he was sitting back in an armchair with his eyes half-closed. It was clear that any questions about exactly what had happened would have to wait.

While Maria Rosa packed her medical bag, Lori looked around the stateroom. It had to have been twice the size of her entire apartment in Manhattan. She looked through large windows to a private deck and, beyond that, to the few lights still on around the marina. A sitting area was furnished with a full-size suede sofa and armchairs, and a small dining table held stacks of magazines and a map of Santa Maria, marked by hand into patches of different colors. On the desk, a laptop blinked stock quotes and other financial news. Lori idly wandered around until she caught Matthew Cunningham's eyes and realized he had been watching her. She looked away and waited for Maria Rosa to finish.

Anton and Lori had not expected any useful information from the Stones, and they got none. Both claimed to know nothing of either Hanson's activities or the altercation on the dock that night. "Good luck finding that crewman," Harold Stone called out with false joviality as they walked away.

Lori said quietly. "Anton, we have no idea where Jack Hanson is."

He drew himself up. "Anton knows. Jack is on Santa Maria, on my island. Anton will find Jack." With that, he balled a hand and thumped it on the rail of the ship. "Anton *will* find Jack."

9

Especially in a small, close-knit community, tension begets tension. Catarina's phone and all three of Anton's phones had been ringing since early morning. Whether because he had been so closely involved with the incident that left a violent drug dealer loose on their island or simply because he was the sort of man who people turn to for help, the expectation was that Anton knew what was happening and what should be done. That expectation was not unfounded. There have always been those whose gift of leadership goes unrecognized until crisis demands it, and they step up. Anton was one of them.

At 10 a.m., he had already been awake for twenty-four hours and was likely to remain awake for another twenty-four. The night before, he had gathered the four policemen of Santa Maria and, assuming authority he was well aware he did not have, he laid out his plan for Hanson's capture. Going on the assumption that a man unused to living rough would not make it to the wilder, less populated regions of the interior or even to nearby towns overnight, he put each of the four in charge of a different area around the marina. They were to enlist the help of citizens and go door to door, alert to anything that seemed suspicious. At the same time, the groups were to search all public places where the fugitive might be hiding. The owner of the café where Hanson had wanted to meet Lori, along with his brother, were deputized and ready to act on a plan Felipe had devised.

Catarina and Lori also had roles to play in locating Jack Hanson and keeping him from harming anyone on Santa Maria. Using the school directory, Catarina called the parents of every student, conveying both the urgency of the situation and a sense of calm as she explained what had happened and asked the same questions Felipe and his men were asking. She had an additional reason for calling the parents. Making it seem almost like an aside from a concerned mother, she talked about possible drug use among the older students, slipping in a question about any teenage boys who might have been buying drugs late the night before. As expected, she started her day with an unmarked notebook and ended five hours later with several pages filled with information to share with Anton.

Lori called Captain Sullivan to get information from Hanson's work papers, and then scoured the Internet for any mention of him. What she found seemed to corroborate Anton's fears. Jack Hanson had first appeared in the weekly crime report of a small city newspaper in Ohio. He had been remanded to the juvenile authorities for robbing houses in his neighborhood. Although those records had been sealed by court order, his parents had very publically fought—and successfully overturned—the consequences meted out by the justice system. Before he was out of his teens, he had been in trouble with the law two more times, both for selling drugs. Over the past four years, he had been arrested and tried for possession of large quantities of OxyContin, but each case had been dismissed on technicalities. The articles Lori read noted that the drug was as dangerous as heroin and more addictive, and it was becoming a major problem among young people and older women, in particular. She could see Hanson's looks and personality having great appeal to those two groups.

By early afternoon, Anton had been in and out of the house five times. Each time Catarina sent him to take a much-needed nap, one of his phones rang and he dashed off again to follow up on leads with Felipe, to distribute copies of Hanson's picture, or to talk with authorities at several marinas on the island. He knew he was now dealing with two serious problems, a murder and a drug dealer loose on the island, and he struggled with whether or not to alert the Judicial Police on São Miguel. He weighed the help they might bring against the impression visitors might get from the presence of armed police at the airport, on the roads, and in the villages, and he decided to give Santa Maria more time to deal with the situation itself.

By 3 p.m., he had reached the end of what he could do about Jack Hanson for the moment, and his thoughts turned to Frank Dekker's murder. He set out for Water's Edge, this time with a different mindset. He was going to do more than simply chat with the people there; he was going to interrogate them in the way Catarina's British detectives did.

At that time, lunch was over and dinner would not start for another five hours, so the restaurant was deserted. He left Catarina, who was to act as his assistant, to settle in at the table closest to the kitchen, and he walked back to where Manuel usually served the men who came to drink. After his eyes adjusted to the dark, it was easy to see this was the oldest of the three rooms at Water's Edge, the place the first Costa and the first Dekker had built to sell the wine they made. A long bar, cobbled together from three thick planks of wood over a hundred and fifty years before, was dark and worn smooth. Glasses of various sizes and shapes packed two shelves in no order whatsoever, and the kegs waiting to fill them sat on a table in the corner.

Two tiny windows, separated by a door with a simple iron latch, were the only source of light. Anton walked out the door to a small area with benches set on a dirt floor. Just beyond, the land dropped off, and he could see across the divide to a grassy green hill with an old dairy: Casa do Mar. Fifty feet below, between the two cliffs, was Farewell Beach, where Frank Dekker's body had been found. Poking around the juniper bushes, he found what he was looking for. Carved into the stone were steps that led down to the cove where the first patrons of Water's Edge had set out to sea after warming themselves on wine from the owners' failing vineyards.

Anton returned to the restaurant and followed the sounds coming from the kitchen. There he found Matias, Manuel, and Isabella sitting around a large table, talking quietly. He heard himself speak with authority. "I want to speak with each of you. It can be either here or at the police station."

They looked at each other. Matias spoke first, "We are getting ready for the evening meal."

"So it would be more convenient here, I take it?"

Matias looked trapped. "Yes."

"I will start with Mrs. Dekker."

Manuel scraped his chair back and glared at Anton defiantly. "She is not well. Can't you see?"

It was true. She did not look well. She was much paler than she had been on the morning he told her of her husband's death, and the skin around her eyes looked bruised. Anton felt his resolve slipping. He didn't want to make the woman's life any harder. He wasn't that sort of man. He spoke more gently, "I have just a few questions. It won't take long at all."

Manuel looked daggers at him, but Isabella laid a hand on his arm. "I'm fine," she said, and she slowly walked into the restaurant.

Catarina was waiting, looking quite businesslike with her pad of paper and pencil neatly laid out in front of her. Anton pulled out a chair for Isabella, who dropped into it with a sigh. He sat beside her, ready to ask his questions and to watch as she reacted. He was glad, however, to have his wife with him; she had better insight into people's emotions than he did.

Before Anton could say a word, Catarina asked, "Would you like some tea or perhaps a small glass of wine?"

Not making eye contact, Isabella shook her head to say no.

Catarina could see the woman was less at ease than when they last met, and certainly unhappier than Lori had described her the day after her husband died. "How are you doing?" she asked.

There was little emotion behind Isabella's weak smile. "I am well."

Anton was blunt. "We are now certain your husband's death was caused by someone else."

Isabella flinched. The arteries in her neck started pulsing rapidly.

"You understand that we must do everything we can to find out who is responsible."

Her nod was slow.

"Did your husband have enemies, *a senhora?*" he asked.

"No one I know of," she said. "I think it must have been a stranger who killed him."

It was the first time anyone had mentioned a stranger. "Had he angered someone that night?"

She shrugged.

"Did he have a lot of money with him?" he asked.

"He may have had the money from Water's Edge that night. Perhaps that's why he was killed."

Anton didn't need help from anyone to know she didn't believe what she had just said. "Is there any money missing?"

Isabella could see the illogic of what she had said. "It was just an idea. I was wrong."

Anton glanced in the direction of the kitchen. Someone had opened the door a crack and was listening.

"Were you working that night?"

"I work every night until midnight."

"So someone at Water's Edge would have seen you all night?"

The door to the kitchen swung open with force, and Manuel came over. Catarina thought he looked even more ashen and stooped than when she and Lori had had lunch there two days earlier. Something was taking a toll on the people of Water's Edge, but it didn't seem to be grief over the loss of Frank Dekker.

"I've already told you," Manuel said hoarsely. She is never out of my sight. We are never out of each other's sight." He helped her to stand. "This is enough for her," he said to Anton.

As he escorted Isabella to the kitchen, Anton said firmly, "After she is settled, please return so we can talk."

121

In the few minutes they waited, Anton and Catarina agreed Isabella was at least withholding information, perhaps even guilty of killing her husband. Either way, she was deeply troubled by something.

Before he even sat down, Manuel repeated what he had said in the kitchen, "She is not well."

Catarina saw that her husband's face had taken on an atypically stern expression. She knew he was forcing himself not to show pity for the people he was questioning, and she knew his approach was not going to work in this situation. Just as he opened his mouth to speak, she jumped in. "This must be so hard on her."

Manuel knew he had an ally, and he visibly relaxed. "Yes. Yes, it is. She's a vulnerable woman."

Catarina continued, while Anton looked on attentively. "Sometimes, your grief doesn't show until later."

Manuel nodded but with reservation. He didn't appear to accept her explanation. Still, he said, "She's been more upset in the past day or two than she was at first."

Catarina couldn't tell whether he offered that to explain why Isabella should be left alone or as evidence of her innocence, or for a reason she was unaware of.

Anton asked, "And you can verify that she was here until midnight on the evening that your brother died?"

With that, Manuel's antagonism returned. "As I said, we are always within sight of each other."

Of course, Anton understood that provided Manuel with an alibi as much as it did Isabella. He moved from opportunity to motive. "Do you know of anyone who might have had reason to kill your brother?"

His response was slow in coming. "No."

While Anton thought for a moment, Catarina asked, "Are things very different without Frank here?"

"Not really. His heart was never in this place, not like our father or Matias. He spent most of his time in what we call *the first room*." He lifted his chin in the direction of the old room Anton had just seen.

Manuel had missed the point of what she wanted to ask. She tried again. "Have the others missed him?"

"Frank didn't have the ...," he brought the tips of his forefingers together, "... bond to people here that others do."

"Surely he had a bond to Isabella and Paolo."

Manuel's *hmm* actually told Catarina quite a lot.

Anton was stymied. The answers he kept getting from the people at Water's Edge didn't allow him to delve into Frank Dekker's death any further. It crossed his mind that he might have better luck returning to Wit's End to question the Cunninghams, and that thought led him to ask Manuel something he hadn't asked about before, "Did you happen to see Frank with any Americans recently, perhaps in the past two weeks, perhaps talking business?"

Manuel was clearly surprised that Anton knew about such a meeting. "Yes. I think I know who you are talking about—brown hair and eyes, light skin but tanned, a well-groomed man." His description could have fit either Cunningham or Stone. "He came two—no three—days before Frank died. He brought a stack of papers to Water's Edge and was showing them to Frank."

Cunningham wasn't in the Azores yet, thought Anton. "Did you hear what they were talking about?"

Manuel searched his memory. "Come to think of it, I had gone into the kitchen, and I heard them arguing. When I came out to see what was happening, they got very quiet. So, no, I didn't hear what they were saying." Without being told there were no further questions, he got up and started back to the kitchen. "Do you want to talk to Matias now?"

By this time, the questions had become routine. With Matias, Anton led with what everyone else seemed most reluctant to answer fully. "How will Isabella's life be different now that Frank is dead?"

"Frank expected a lot ...." He stopped to think about something.

Anton was about to ask his next question, but Catarina cautioned him with her eyes. She knew you could learn a lot about a person by simply listening to whatever they chose to talk about.

"Frank never appreciated his wife," Matias finally said.

"In which way?" Anton asked.

"She brings so much to Water's Edge. She understands the value of tradition."

Catarina heard the strong feelings in his voice. She knew that—uninterrupted—he would lose himself in his passion and continue talking about what he loved.

"She is proud that this place has come to us through our ancestors, in an unbroken line for almost two hundred years. She is proud of how sacrifice and hard work and honor have led to this." He laid a hand on the glass-fronted cabinet next to his chair. "She cares for our history as I do."

Anton followed Matias' gaze to the cabinet with shelves holding memorabilia and had to suppress a gasp. He made an immediate connection between what he saw and the morning on Farewell Beach, when he stood beside Frank Dekker's body. Small wood carvings, embellished with beautifully-rendered porcelain figures, filled one shelf. "Who made these?" he asked, barely able to keep his voice steady.

Matias beamed. "Each one was made by both the first Costa and the first Dekker to own Water's Edge." He reached under his shirt and pulled out a crucifix identical to the one found near Frank's body. "One of these was made for the first Costa son and the other for the first Dekker son, and they've been passed down through the generations. My father gave me his just before he died. Frank's father left him his, but I don't think Frank ever wore it. It belongs to Paolo now."

Anton's heart was pounding. "I feel like I've seen that before. Where is the other one?"

Matias grew red in the face and quickly stuffed the crucifix back under his shirt. To Catarina it was clear that he regretted being carried away by his feelings and saying too much.

It was hard for Anton not to press for an answer to his question, but he had already learned something from his wife's approach to getting information from people. He sat still and waited until it became clear that Matias had either forgotten what he was asked or wanted to avoid answering. He repeated, "Where is the other one?"

Matias stumbled over his words as he said, "I haven't seen it in a long time."

"Where was it the last time you saw it."

"I can't remember exactly."

"Matias, can you think of anyone who might have wanted Frank dead?"

"Truly, my friend, I know of no one who would kill Frank."

Anton was not at all reassured by what he heard. Like Lori, he had started to think he was getting honest answers that were intended to lead him astray. Listening carefully to Matias, it dawned on him that he had asked one question but received an answer to another, slightly different question—and not for the first time in his investigation. It was a small difference, true, and could have been unintentional, but Anton knew how his friend valued telling the truth. *Could he believe someone did want Frank Dekker dead but not believe that person was capable of murder? Could he be wrong about that person's innocence?*

With Anton working late at the office and the children sleeping with their friends across the road, Lori and Catarina spent a quiet evening in the Casa do Mar kitchen, sipping cups of hot cocoa and talking through the visit from the Gillis Foundation in just five days.

Beto was wrapping up the work on Casa do Bosque, and the landscapers, two brothers who shared a nearby fig orchard, had dug holes for the last rose bushes that were waiting to be planted. Anton's solution to the missing drainage pipes had been inspired: there were none. Shiny new drains in the bathroom led absolutely nowhere. In case someone should turn on the water, a large rubber tube led from each drain to a barrel just outside the wall.

Catarina was finishing a small watercolor to hang at the entrance of Casa do Bosque. They had all watched as she roughed in the new guest house against its backdrop of wild ocean and awe-inspiring cliffs but as the details emerged, she shooed them away. She wanted the final work to be a surprise.

One unsurmountable problem remained. They had not found a way to get their visitors to Santa Maria any earlier than Monday. Anton would have to meet them in Ponta Delgada on Sunday and stay there with them until the first available flight at noon the next day. That would not showcase everything that was special about Santa Maria, and it would leave just under two hours to see the land they were being asked to conserve and all the work that had been done at Casa do Mar. It was not auspicious.

As she walked through the dark barn that night, Lori ran through the visit in her mind. *Should they skip the tour of the island? How much time should they spend at Casa do Mar? Which points of the proposal should be discussed?*

Lori was lost in the sounds of the old barn, the sighing of the wind under its roof, the dripping of a water tap into an old tin sink, the faint applause of the leaves just outside the windows, the creaking of wood as it cooled in the night air.

The defenses she had learned living in New York City had faded. She should not have ignored the open window. She should have noticed the shadow changing shape against one of the milking stalls. She should have returned to the kitchen.

The danger appeared suddenly. A man jumped in front of her, three feet away, shining a flashlight in her eyes. Blinded, she turned back to the kitchen and started to run, but her legs were kicked out from under her. As she fell, her flashlight went flying out of her hand.

She scrambled up and steadied herself against a wall, but he lunged at her, and she found herself face down on a bale of hay.

She spun around, kicking wildly, trying to keep him away, but her legs met empty air. There was no one there. Lori got to her feet, spat hay out of her mouth, and hoarsely called out to Catarina.

Without warning, the shadowy figure knocked her down again, this time back-first to the hard wood floor. Her neck snapped. She couldn't take a breath. For several seconds, she struggled to get up, only to have her attacker stomp her down again and again. There was no time to think through a defense, no time to even process what was happening to her. She was becoming disoriented. Instinctively, she covered her head with her arms and managed to take in a couple of breaths of dusty air.

She was in luck. Her flashlight had landed between two hay bales, pointing up. As her vision cleared, she was able to see a leg as it came toward her. She grabbed at it. He shook her loose but stumbled backward. While he tried to get his balance, Lori jumped up and ran.

He started hurling things at her—a bucket, a stool, a jar of nails. A spade hit her in the head. She staggered away, stunned. The figure was moving at her with a shovel.

Catarina's voice came from the doorway. "What is the noise? Is everything alright?"

It was then that Lori's attacker made his mistake. He turned towards Catarina.

Lori leapt into a milking stall and felt around for a weapon.

Catarina came running with a fierce cry, grabbing a pitchfork as she came. Lori was able to find a heavy milk can in the dim light. With all her remaining strength, she hoisted it overhead and hurled it at the indistinct figure. It caught him on a shoulder, he lost his footing, and fell against a wall. Without Catarina closing in on him, the unknown attacker headed toward a side door and melted into the darkness.

Lori stumbled to Catarina's side and collapsed, shaking uncontrollably. Catarina knelt beside her and cradled her head in her lap. "He's gone. You are safe."

"What made you come?"

"Someone has to take care of you," she said, stroking her hair.

"Someone has to take care of you, too," Lori said, nestling closer into Catarina's lap.

"Anton and I take care of each other."

I've never really had someone to take care of me, Lori thought, and for the first time she could remember, she cried.

There had been love in Lori Moore's home; it just hadn't been love for her.

Her parents had met at college and bonded immediately, tightly, and permanently as they became involved with the social upheavals of the 1960s. They had protested the draft together; they had marched on Washington together; they had experimented with drugs together; they had moved to New Hampshire together. Over time, they changed; some would say they had outgrown the lifestyle that had brought them together. Harmony Moore had returned to her birth name of Hannah and—like Catarina's mother—had earned her nursing degree. George Moore had started as a copywriter at a textbook firm and worked his way up to middle management. They had moved from their rented apartment and taken on the mortgage for a small house in Manchester, where they hung curtains, painted rooms, and planted trees.

Lori was born to them after they had been together for seventeen years and had made a life that satisfied them. They supported her and if asked, they would have said they did love her. It was just not the love a child craves. She knew she was not special to them. Their lives would have been as good, as complete, without her.

When her parents retired, it was to a one-bedroom condominium in Florida, one to which Lori was never invited to spend a night on the sofa. So as a teen, she spent college vacations either with friends' families or in various summer programs. After graduation, she saw her parents once a year, when she visited Florida. She learned to be a family of one.

She hadn't even been sure she was missing anything—until she arrived at Casa do Mar.

"I want to tell you what brought me here," Lori said with no introduction whatsoever.

Catarina had wrapped her shawl around a still-trembling Lori, and they were sitting at the kitchen table, hands around large cups of tea they were not drinking. From the moment she first saw her American guest, Catarina had sensed her loneliness. She said nothing but gave Lori her full attention.

Lori told her about the work she had done and how she had put an end to any possibility of returning to that life.

"Does that make you unhappy?" Catarina asked.

"No." Lori surprised herself with the assurance of her answer. "No," she repeated, sorting out her thoughts as she spoke, "I really wasn't happy doing what I was doing. I should have been, but I wasn't."

"Why do you say you *should* have been happy?"

"I had so much. I know that. A person should be grateful for a place to live, and food, and clothes. I had more—not just a comfortable place to live but one filled with all sorts of things other people want but can't afford, not just nutritious food but meals in fine restaurants, not just clothes but so many of the best clothes."

"You had more," Catarina said quietly, "and less." Memories of her own childhood crossed her mind.

Lori held her breath waiting to understand why she had never felt she had enough, when she had so much. "What do you mean?"

"Let me ask you, what do think Anton wants to accomplish here on Santa Maria?"

The answer seemed straightforward. "He wants to preserve his—your—culture."

"Anton understands the tension between allowing a culture to move forward and preserving it. He knows that progress is essential to employment and medical care and education, but he also knows that progress usually comes at the cost of traditional culture. Your society paid that cost and in doing so, you lost so much."

Lori knew there was truth in what Catarina was saying. Despite what they did not have, most people on Santa Maria seemed happier than the people whose paths she had crossed in Manhattan.

"Village life has nurtured our people for five hundred years. Our social ties make us a large extended family, with people bonded to each other in many ways. That comforts us; more, that gives us pleasure."

Lori thought back to a college course in which the professor said that human beings are not far removed from their primate ancestors, pack animals who were most contented when together in small groups, each individual contributing to a common effort.

"We do not want to preserve our culture simply so some record of it remains. We are not looking for tourists to come and sample our heritage in museums and historic houses, only to find that they are wiping out even more of it. We want our traditions to …," Catarina searched for how to explain it, "… be real, not acted on a stage."

Lori's mind went to sites in Europe and the Americas: cameras clicking during Sunday Mass in Notre Dame, throngs of tourists craning their necks at tableaus in Colonial Williamsburg, hawkers selling plastic replicas of the Coliseum, and always somewhere close by, McDonald's and Starbucks.

What she had seen on Santa Maria *was* different. Dogs romped in pastures; children played ball in village squares; washing hung on lines; music could be heard through open windows. And there was the perfection of imperfection in a neglected plant lying shriveled on the ground or a shutter that hung lopsided or a crumbling wall being reclaimed by vines. Santa Maria was living. It was *real*.

"We are not ...," Catarina continued. "What is the expression? ... *starry-eyed*. We know historical conservation is not a solution for all the problems of the world, and," she smiled, "we do want to enjoy some of the advantages of living in the twenty-first century. Anton only means to preserve a more traditional way of life for those who are sustained by it." Thinking of her beloved husband brought a tear to her eyes. "It has always been Anton's gift that he cares more about others than about himself."

"You have that quality, too."

"Then we are a trio, my friend. Remember what has made you part of our lives."

Lori's thoughts came together slowly, quietly. I am *happy* here.

10

Arguably, the attack in the barn affected Anton more than it had Lori.

He questioned his motives in trying to find a person, perhaps two people, who had committed serious crimes. *Am I putting people at risk just to serve* my *ambitions?* He thought through the progress—or lack of progress—he had been able to make with only four police officers, none of them experienced in such matters. *I have been playing at being a detective.*

And now, I have jeopardized the safety of my own family.

He decided on the best way to bring in Pedro Medina and the Judicial Police on São Miguel without causing trouble for Felipe and his men. As Catarina looked on, he took out his personal cell phone. "Darling, I must take full responsibility for not having informed the Judicial Police immediately. This will probably mean an end to my appointment ... an end to ... everything." He clenched his jaw tight. "I am so sorry, Catarina. I will make this up to you, to our family."

She came up behind him and rested her hands on his broad shoulders. He felt her warmth through his shirt, reassuring him that she would always be with him and giving him an undefined hope for their future.

He made the call and asked to be put through to Pedro Medina.

Catarina reached over, slipped the phone from his hand, and pressed the red button. "No," she said, her voice the most gentle and the most firm it had ever been.

Anton turned his head to question her.

"No," she repeated. "*No* for us—*no* for our neighbors, *no* for everyone on Santa Maria. We must try to end this quietly before the outside world comes to think of us in a way we are not, and we lose the chance to keep what we have."

He was so tired. He tried to think through what would be best for everyone he cared for, but his thoughts hung in a fog. He searched his wife's face for answers.

"One more day," she said resolutely.

He couldn't think of any words to resist her. He drew a deep breath and shuddered. "Just one day. Any longer, and Hanson may get more desperate. The person who murdered Frank Dekker may slip away or do even more damage. The risk will be too great."

Lori found the couple sitting in silence, sipping coffee. Anton immediately got to his feet, wrapped his strong arms around her, and pressed her to him protectively. Her tears wet his shirt, but they did not come from any lingering fear or relief; they came from feeling so loved.

Anton looked at her face, swollen with two black eyes and a gash across her forehead where the spade had hit. He hung his head. "Sorry, Lori. All Santa Maria sorry."

When the children came for breakfast, Lori learned the healing touch children can bring. Liliana, her mother's daughter, gently laid a hand—delicate as a butterfly wing—on each of Lori's wounds. "It hurts a lot?"

"It's not too bad."

"You need cold to make ...," she did not know the word for swelling, "... the bigness get smaller."

Before Lori had the time to agree, Liliana went to the sink and got a wet cloth to put on her face. Behind the dark damp, she heard Toni tease her. "Lori is *Super Lori* to fight bad man! I will tell Nuno about *Super Lori*."

Anton had slept only a few hours since Hanson's escape, two and a half days earlier, and Catarina could tell her husband was almost numb from exhaustion. She led him to their bedroom by the hand, took off his rumpled suit and shirt, and told him to take a long nap before returning to his office. She confiscated all three of his cell phones and, as she walked away, assured him she would check frequently to make sure he was actually sleeping.

Maria Rosa arrived with her medical bag to check Lori's injuries. Toni looked on with great interest and asked to help apply the antibiotic ointment to the long cut on Lori's forehead, which he did tenderly and capably.

"Maybe you will be a doctor one day," said Lori.

"Yes. I will," the eight-year-old said confidently. He was his father's son.

Lori kissed the top of his head and whispered, "Thank you," into his dark brown curls. She was thanking everyone around her for accepting her as one of their own.

After Maria Rosa took the children to school, Lori and Catarina talked about what had happened in the barn the night before, this time to see if they could identify the attacker. Neither could. It seemed most likely, they agreed, that it was Hanson, since Lori's phone was the best evidence against him, and he would want to get rid of it—and possibly her. The shadowy figure had the right build to be Jack Hanson, but so did many other men. They considered other possibilities for the attack. Could Lori have been told or overheard something as she acted as Anton's interpreter? Could her video have captured something they were unaware of? Could it have been an act of revenge?

What they did not talk about was what actually troubled them most. *If the attacker did not get what he came for, would he return?*

When useful information finally came, it came suddenly and from unexpected sources.

Toni was the first to burst through the school's front door. He ran up to his mother, followed by his friend, Nuno. A woman with a friendly smile joined them. "This is Nuno's mama," he said. Catarina and Lori recognized her as the waitress from Water's Edge.

The three adults exchanged greetings and settled on the low stone wall that bordered the schoolyard. As is customary in many social settings, the conversation started with inquiries about children, observations on the weather, and talk about upcoming community events, including the annual football matches between island teams to be held the next day.

Then Catarina asked Estela if she had time for a few questions. "A man is dead, murdered, here on our own island," she began in English. "If we are going to find the person who did it, we need information from someone we can trust to give honest answers."

Lori listened to Catarina's approach to getting information, different from Anton's. After talking about personal connections, she had let Estela know that this was something they needed to collaborate on, something for their common good.

"Have you noticed any changes at Water's Edge, now that Frank is dead?" It was a question that had been asked without success before.

Estela's first response was much the same as everyone else's had been. "He was never around enough for there to be a difference."

Catarina was able to take the process more slowly than Anton had. She knew everyone was being vague, perhaps because there was nothing specific to point to but perhaps intentionally. Rather than suffer Anton's frustration, she backed away and started talking—almost to herself—about how difficult it must be to raise children without the support of family and friends. Then, as a statement rather than a question, she circled back, "It must be especially hard for Isabella now that Frank is dead."

Estela looked almost amused. Catarina said nothing and waited to hear more. She did. "Frank was not the best husband. She is probably better off without him."

"In which way was he not *the best?*"

Estela took her time before whispering. "Frank wasn't a good man," she said slowly. "He was unhappy, and he blamed everyone around him for that, especially Isabella."

"And how was he with Paolo?"

"Now that was strange. He completely ignored the boy, paid him less attention than a guest at the restaurant did ...," her voice trailed off as she confirmed a conclusion to herself, "... except when Isabella was around. Then, he would put Paolo on his shoulders and tickle him and talk about how they were going to America one day."

"Does anyone miss Frank?"

"Not that I know of."

Again, Catarina changed to an unrelated subject for a few minutes. She didn't want their conversation to become an interrogation. "I can pick up Nuno tomorrow, so the boys can play for a while before Anton starts the warm-up for the match." Catarina laughed quietly thinking about her husband's role as coach of a local team. "He would be happy to play football for a living. I think he secretly dreams of being another Christian Rinaldo," she said, naming the most famous of all Azorean footballers.

After the two mothers shared a laugh at Anton's expense and arranged for their sons to get together the next day, Catarina said, "I know Anton was wondering about the American who came to talk to Frank two or three days before he died." She said no more and left Estela to fill the silence that followed.

The young woman pulled her thoughts together and asked, "Do you mean the man who went into the restaurant or the woman who stayed on the road?"

Catarina raised her eyebrows. "An American woman was there, too?"

"I had parked along the side of the road as usual, and I was taking my time before going in to work. You know how it is with children; there's so much mess. I was clearing out trash from the car and wiping down the seats."

Catarina nodded but said nothing.

"The man and woman were leaning against their car—I'm sorry I can't describe them well. The woman was small and blond from a bottle, and she wore a large white hat. All I remember about the man was that he was dressed like a magazine model but not young or handsome."

Although Estela had switched to a mix of Portuguese and English, Lori understood. She needed no further description; she was certain they were the Stones.

"They were both, you know, people who find fault with so much in their lives," Estela continued.

Catarina showed she understood with a simple *mm-hmm*.

"They probably didn't realize that I know some English—or maybe they simply didn't care about someone on Santa Maria hearing them. The woman was angry. She was talking rather loudly, saying she *never agreed to this*. She complained about everything she had been promised but never gotten."

That certainly sounds like Eleanor Stone, thought Lori.

"The man said someone was going to make sure everything would be fine soon." Estela looked at Catarina. "I wish I could tell you more. I just had the impression that something important was going to happen, and he thought that would make the woman happy."

"Did that seem to satisfy the woman?" prompted Catarina.

"No," she said, trying hard to remember more. "In fact, she sounded like she was scolding the man. She wasn't going *to lose it all.*" Estela chuckled. "I hate to say it, but the whole conversation was sort of interesting, like watching a soap opera on television."

The older children were coming out of school, and both women started to watch for their daughters. With what was happening on the island, all the parents were more vigilant than they ever thought they would have to be.

Lori thought of one more question as Estela walked away. "Did you see the man after he went into the restaurant?" she called out after her.

Estela stopped and turned around. "Oh, yes. He and Frank were talking ...," she slowed a bit, thinking there was significance in what she was saying, "... actually, more arguing than talking." She stared at the ground as one by one, disconnected memories returned. "They seemed to reach some agreement. They shook hands. Matias came in. They all went out to the back patio, and the arguing began all over again." She looked up at Lori, pleased and nodding. "Yes. That *is* what happened."

Estela laughed. "Then I had to stop watching the drama and start working. I hope that helped." She took her daughter's hand, told her son it was time to get in the car, and waved goodbye.

Lori and Catarina made eye contact and smiled at each other.

The call came in the early hours of the morning. Jack Hanson had been found trying to bribe a fisherman to take him across the strait to São Miguel. The fisherman had tackled him then and there, and called the police. When Felipe arrived at the marina, he found Hanson in the hold of a boat, tied up and squirming in a slick of fish guts.

Anton had only just fallen asleep. The ringing phone woke up all three adults, none of whom were resting easily after the attack in the barn. By this time, they knew each other well enough for Lori to get ready to accompany Anton without being asked, and for Catarina to make coffee for them before they left.

When they arrived at the police station, Anton, Felipe, and Lori had a short meeting in the hallway. They decided to build their case against Hanson slowly, letting him react to their initial accusations before showing him the video Lori had made from the ferry deck. Along with the video, the people being driven in by the remaining three members of the Santa Maria Police Department would leave him little way to avoid a conviction for selling drugs. Anton and Felipe were to go into the room first, talk to one another in Portuguese, and completely ignore the prisoner. Then Lori would enter, the only person he could communicate with, a fellow American who had some sympathy for him. As Felipe said, it would make Hanson more likely to trust what she said.

When Anton and Felipe entered, the prisoner was still tied up hand and foot by a length of rope that could have restrained four men. He reeked of rotting fish.

"You want to untie me here?" he yelled angrily when they came in. "That idiot fisherman violated my civil rights. He's not even a cop."

Neither Anton nor Felipe gave any indication they had heard him.

"Hey. Get me out of these ropes."

Felipe loudly scraped a chair across the floor and sat by the door, stony-faced. Anton picked up a folder and slowly leafed through the papers inside, shaking his head and judgmentally raising his eyebrows at Hanson from time to time, as though he was reading the record of a particularly reprehensible criminal. The folder actually held the monthly bills for the police station.

After five minutes or so, Lori came in. She feigned surprise at seeing Hanson.

"What are you doing here?" he asked.

"Oh," she said slowly, "I remember you. Your black eye is almost gone." She took a deep slow breath. "You are being detained for selling drugs on the island of Santa Maria." She sounded unemotional, as though she was reluctantly reciting a prepared statement. "What is your response to that charge?" She ended with a weak smile intended to show some regret for the role she was playing.

Hanson loudly denied he had ever sold drugs.

"Apparently, Captain Sullivan and his daughter are willing to testify against you."

His eyes flickered with fear before he became confrontational again. "It's their word against mine."

"Others could confirm what they say." *I'm not saying others actually did confirm it.*

He dismissed that with scorn. "They've still got no *proof.*"

"The police have taken possession of a video I made. While I was filming boats in the harbor, I happened to capture you in the background. They want to show it to you."

When Anton slammed a laptop on the desk, Hanson jerked helplessly in his rope sheath, and when Anton glared while showing the transaction on the dock, Hanson did his unsuccessful best to shrink away.

He tried to challenge Anton, but his voice wobbled, "That could be anything I'm selling."

Without saying a word, Felipe stepped out into the hall and returned, leading the three teens from the video, identified thanks to Catarina's conversations with parents at the school.

"Jack, it seems like they have a lot of words against your one," said Lori with insincere regret.

"It's just a few harmless pills. No big deal."

Lori lowered her voice, as though she was taking Hanson into her confidence. "Jack, the justice system here is swift and firm. I know Minister Cardosa. He is the emissary of the President himself. His powers are far-reaching. There will be no extradition. There will be no mercy."

His face blanched, and his jaw slackened.

Anton, Felipe, and Lori had agreed it would be best to start by confronting Hanson with the compelling evidence against him in the drug sale, but that was not the only crime he was implicated in. They also wanted to hear everything he knew about the attack at Casa do Mar and about Frank Dekker's death.

"Minister Cardosa is very concerned with violence on Santa Maria, and about the murder of one of its citizens," she said gently.

"Murder?" Hanson squeaked, almost making it to his feet before he reached the end of his long rope and rebounded to the chair. "Murder? I didn't murder no one. I don't do crap like that."

He looked almost pathetic enough for her to believe him.

"Who'm I supposed to have murdered?" He was close to screaming.

"Mr. Frank Dekker was murdered on the night of April 3rd."

"The third? The third? That was Friday. I wasn't even here. We didn't even dock until Saturday."

"There's more than one way to get onto Santa Maria, Mr. Hanson, and *Wit's End* was in São Miguel for several days before that. The police will certainly want to know exactly where you were that night."

"Yeah," he searched his memory and tried to reconstruct the timeline. "Yeah. We docked in São Miguel the Tuesday before. That would be the … 31st. I … I was on second shift … so I had to do the refuel when we got in and … okay, I remember … then I had to check everyone on shore leave back in. That went on until midnight."

Lori glanced at Felipe, who was taking notes. "What about the other days?"

Hanson took a deep breath. "Let's see. Oh yeah, on Wednesday we took the ship around the island. All hands on deck." Lori looked at Felipe again. "Thursday … um … Thursday …." He looked worried. "I got it! How could I forget? It was monthly maintenance day. Among other things, I was pouring vinegar down all the heads." He grimaced. "Then we left for Santa Maria late on Friday." He looked victorious. "I couldn't have murdered no one. I was in the middle of the ocean."

Felipe got up to call Captain Sullivan and check on what Hanson had said.

Lori was glad the interrogation had turned to murder first; it had left Hanson rattled and more willing to admit to other things. "Even if that checks out, Jack, the penalty for attacking me will be ...." She grimly shook her head.

"Attacking you?" There was a marked difference between his reaction to that accusation and his reaction when he thought he was being accused of murder. She knew he was the one.

Lori was pleased with her next little invention. "Well, clearly you aren't aware of a surveillance system at Casa do Mar." *I didn't say there is one.*

Tired, thirsty, and under suspicion for murder, Hanson was reaching a point of panic.

"How did you know where I would be, anyway?" she asked. His smile was so close to smug, Lori had a hard time resisting an urge to throw the nearest heavy object at him.

"People like talking to me. I asked around. You could hardly be missed. You're the tallest, blondest woman on this entire island."

Lori had had enough. She decided to drive home her advantage. "I don't know exactly what prison conditions are in the Azores, but it won't be like in America. I don't even know if there is time off for good behavior, and the sentence could be ...." She left that hanging and let out an audible breath.

"I just wanted your cell phone," he said angrily. "What gives you the right to video other people, anyway?"

Amazing. Now it's my fault.

Hanson rethought his strategy. "I wasn't going to hurt you. You were the one who had to fight me for it."

Anton punched one hand with the other. Angry, he was a terrifying presence, upturned mouth or not.

Jack had taken notice. "Look, let's not go all crazy with this. Maybe I can help you. Show you I'm not such a bad guy." He gave Lori his best, toothy white smile.

Unbelievable. He's actually trying to flirt his way out of this.

Getting no response from Lori, Hanson stopped straining against his rope and assumed a blank expression. "This Frank Dekker, he's a round guy with red hair, right?"

Anton nodded slowly.

"I know something about him, but if I'm going to help you, you gotta help me."

"What is it that you think will be of use to the police? Whether or not the Minister decides to help you will depend on how much you help him."

Hanson was stuck. He would have to give up what he knew for the chance of a lighter sentence. He tried again. "I want ...." He didn't know what he should ask for.

It didn't matter. Lori cut in, using her own charms, "I understand what you've been saying, Jack," she said softly. "I'll do my best for you." Looking almost cowed by Anton, she asked if he would step out into the hallway with her. Once there, Anton pulled his eyebrows together to ask what she wanted. "We wait," she said. "We wait." Anton nodded with a smile on his face.

Together, they slowly sipped cups of hot tea, made by the mother of one of the boys brought in by the police. In fact, the station was as crowded as it had ever been, with the extended family of all three teens standing around, talking, or playing cards. Occasionally, Anton would shout out, "No!" loud enough to be heard by Hanson, who twitched in his chair each time.

Finally, Lori positioned herself by the door to the room where he was being held and said loudly, "Thank you, Minister, thank you so much."

Once they had settled inside, she drew a deep breath and said gravely, "Minister Plenipotentiary Cardosa has generously agreed to the following. You will tell Chief of Police ...," she hesitated. She didn't know Felipe's last name. She made one up, "... Aragon everything you know. If it proves useful, Minister Cardosa will sign and seal a statement indicating that you gave this information and that it can be taken into account during sentencing." She had just told him that he would be found guilty and had not actually agreed to anything Anton was not in a position to offer. Her earnest delivery was impeccable. Virtually anyone hearing her speech would have thought she was completely on Jack Hanson's side.

None-too-bright, it took Hanson less than thirty seconds to start talking. "Harold Stone met with Frank Dekker on São Miguel. I was having a smoke on the dock, waiting to sign in the last of the crew the night we got in. I saw them whispering, so I decided to listen. You never know when something is going to be useful, do you?" He congratulated himself on his foresight.

"Just tell the Minister what you heard," she prompted, worried that he might have a change of heart if he got sidetracked.

"This Frank Dekker was going to arrange to have some land sold to Stone."

That's all? "I don't think that's going to be enough to make the Minister think your help is worth writing a statement."

"Wait. Wait. There's more. They were going to trick some guy into selling the land for preservation, when really a resort was going to be built on it." He was getting more interesting. "This resort was going to make both of them a lot of money—a lot of ...," he looked at her like he was the cleverest person in the room, "... *untraceable* money."

Now that was more than anyone in the room had expected.

11

It was the day of the annual football matches between the villages of Santa Maria. The spectators that ringed the field where Anton's team would be playing numbered fewer than two hundred, but that was more people than Lori had seen in one place since arriving on Santa Maria. It was a festive crowd. Activities were steeped in tradition: small local bands took turns playing; a folk dancing group practiced for its evening show; and the smell of roasting linguiça filled the air.

Anton was running back and forth with his team, shouting words of encouragement to the young players, but that occupied only the smallest part of his conscious mind. *Wit's End* and everyone aboard her were being detained at the marina. And that was where he was heading the moment the match ended.

Catarina stood with other parents in the shade of trees at the edge of the field. Her mind was not on the match, either. Instead, she was trying to remember what had prodded her the night they had dinner at Water's Edge, but it remained stubbornly just out of reach. She pictured their little group at the restaurant, the warm welcome, Manuel opening the wine, Isabella bringing freshly-baked bread and olive oil, Matias sitting with them at the end of the meal. Something had crossed her mind just as he brought over the cheese platter. *What?*

She tried to recall the conversation they had been having just before it was interrupted by Matias. They had been talking about something they hadn't wanted him to hear. Then were carried away trying to extract information from him. What were they talking about? She remembered.

They were talking about how detectives looked for means, opportunity, and motive. They had decided that everyone had the means—it was an easy thing to pick up a rock from the beach—but no one had much of an opportunity. Then they had discussed motives. There was no gain for Manuel in his brother's death; Matias had wanted to sell the land, just as Frank had; and Isabella would not have made much profit from her husband's death.

Catarina's mind tried to give her clues. The empty space where a wedding picture of Frank and Isabella had once hung came to mind, and then she started to think about her own wedding anniversary in two days. They would celebrate at home, tell a story or two about their courtship to Liliana and Toni, look through old pictures together, and share the traditional anniversary dinner. Anton would give her a small gift, sometimes sweet, sometimes silly, always imaginative and always chosen with love. Love.

Love tickled her mind. She could see Chief Inspector Barnaby sitting in a pub and saying, "It always comes down to two motives: money and *love*."

Catarina grabbed Lori's hand and pulled her aside. "I forgot about love," she said, her cheeks pink with excitement.

Lori stared at her, completely baffled.

"I forgot about love," Catarina repeated. "We talked about money as the motive for Frank's murder. What if it was love?"

Lori grinned. "Yes! Let's say he had another relationship. That woman could have killed him in anger if he was no longer interested, especially if he'd changed his mind about leaving Isabella for her."

"Given what we know about him, it doesn't seem likely that Frank Dekker would be the object of such love."

Lori agreed and offered an alternative. "He could have been killed because he intended to stay in a relationship, a relationship that upset someone else."

"That is more likely."

"Isabella."

"Perhaps ...," Catarina spoke as she thought through the final possibility, "... he could have kept the killer from the person he or she loved."

"That would be Isabella, again. What if she's in love with someone else?"

"To be fair, it could be almost anyone, even the people from *Wit's End*. Mr. Dekker could have seen or heard something on São Miguel or when the Stones went to Water's Edge, something that could have kept two people apart."

"He might have even threatened to tell what he knew."

"Blackmail," Catarina said with a mixture of horror and excitement.

But without more evidence, they could take their thoughts no further and both fell silent.

For no reason she was consciously aware of, Catarina started to think about villages, ones on Santa Maria and others elsewhere. She was thinking aloud when she said, "Villages are much the same the world over."

With even less understanding of what had led to that observation than Catarina herself had, Lori just said, "I suppose."

"Whether clinging to a Greek mountainside, nestled in a Swiss valley, or tucked into a forest, there is the usual joy and sorrow, the usual comedy and drama."

"And the usual evil?"

Catarina was quiet for a few moments. She knew she was getting closer to something important. "Villages are not immune to human frailties, not even the villages of the Azores. There may be less evil in villages, but perhaps it is more readily seen and more keenly felt. It is not masked by great distances between houses or diluted by many thousands of good souls. When it appears, it displays itself fiercely."

Her family had only been part of the community for six weeks, but already Catarina could look around the playing field and see people with rare insight. She could spot the sage and the fool, the clown and the romantic, the busybody who wanted to know everyone's personal business—and the quiet observer who really did.

She saw a couple of the parents whispering to each other, and that was when her thoughts pulled together and she remembered Miss Marple, a detective she was particularly fond of, saying *People in villages love to gossip.* "Lori," she said with urgency, "Estela told us what she is certain of, but people also talk about what they only suspect. Rumors. And often there is truth in a rumor."

Catarina walked over to a small group of teachers and mothers who were about to part company. She returned ten minutes later with an excited look on her face. "We have to talk to Anton. I think we have more suspects now."

Anton and Lori went directly to the marina after the match. By the time they arrived, a sharp wind was coming off a choppy gray ocean, dark purplish clouds had moved in from the Atlantic, and the misted air promised rain. It was a fitting backdrop for what they had to do.

Felipe and his men were waiting on the dock, along with two immigrations officers. Anton led the charge up the gangplank, stationing people along the way so there would be no chance of anyone on board leaving.

Their entrance took the Cunninghams and the Stones by surprise. All four were in the salon off the main deck, sheltered from the light rain that had started to fall. Cunningham closed his laptop before looking up. "Hello, Minister Cardosa. Ms. Moore," he said evenly.

"What's going on here?" Stone was covering fear with indignation. "I understand we are being held against our will."

Eleanor Stone rose from one of the white leather sofas where she was reading a copy of *Architectural Digest* and walked over to her sister, who was sitting at a large, round table and staring at a glossy magazine cover. She addressed Lori, "Carolyn and I will leave you to your business." Mrs. Cunningham looked at her sister without expression and started to get up.

"No," said Anton firmly.

Lori mimicked his tone when she repeated, "No. You are all to remain here while the Minister and the Chief of Police question you." She nodded to Felipe, who—despite not being the Chief of Police—acted the part well with his posture and expression.

Mrs. Cunningham reached up and put a hand on her sister's shoulder, pulling her down to the chair next to her. She looked resigned, but whether to being questioned or something else was not clear.

"The Minister will start by telling you that Jack Hanson, a member of the *Wit's End* crew, has been arrested for selling drugs to young people on Santa Maria."

The reactions were varied and interesting. Matthew Cunningham seemed righteously pleased, his wife appeared close to tears, and Eleanor Stone was clearly irritated. Not unexpectedly, Harold Stone started shouting, "And you're holding us here because someone we didn't even know committed a crime we weren't even aware of?"

Lori continued, "We are not interested in that ... at the moment. We are interested in something he has told us." She addressed the two businessmen, "We want to know more about your interest in purchasing 2000 acres of land on Santa Maria." She had chosen her words carefully. She let them know she was already aware of details and wanted to know *more*.

Cunningham could have been addressing a board meeting at corporate headquarters. "As a global firm with diversified interests, we are always open to acquiring select properties."

"And what is your interest in *this* select property?" Lori confronted them, making eye contact first with one and then the other.

Stone's hostility had vanished, along with his composure. Nervously drumming his fingers against his pants, he looked at Cunningham.

"I recently appointed Harold as my firm's CIO, Chief Investment Officer. He manages our assets portfolio. I rely on him to bring new investment opportunities to the board's attention and in that capacity, he recommended a high-yield investment on Santa Maria—one I was considering."

Stone swallowed hard. He was not happy with what Cunningham was saying.

"Yes, we are aware of his connection to the property," said Lori for the pure pleasure of seeing Stone squirm. Thunder boomed overhead, and she chose that moment to discover how much he knew about the murder. She turned sharply to face Stone and said sarcastically, "Perhaps on further thought, you have reconsidered what you said about having no association with Frank Dekker." She paused for effect, then continued, "What did you and he talk about when you met on São Miguel?"

Cunningham froze in place, his face judgmental. He waited for an answer and, when that didn't come, he said, "Yes, Harold, what *did* you and Frank Dekker talk about?"

"I just thought I would bring him up to speed."

Cunningham pointedly turned his back on everyone and looked out the large salon window. The strong wind buffeting the ship added to the tension in the room, and Lori could see his neck muscles grow rigid. She decided to unsettle Stone further, letting him know they were aware of even more. "I repeat, the Minister wants to hear what you and Frank Dekker talked about when you met in Ponta Delgada on March 31st, and why you chose not to tell us about the meeting before."

"If you knew more about high finance, you would understand why I keep my business opportunities under wraps until the deal is sealed." Neither his words nor the sneer that accompanied them had much conviction behind them.

Cunningham turned around to face Stone. "If—*if*—I approved, that business opportunity would have been between *the firm* and these people, not between *you* and them."

Lori watched as Anton walked over to where the two wives sat, behind them a smudged view of the harbor visible through a pelting rain. Eleanor Stone was still holding the copy of *Architectural Digest* she had been reading. He looked at the magazine, made eye contact with Lori, and nodded almost imperceptibly.

She picked up on what he wanted her to ask. "And that was all? You had no plans to meet him later?"

"None whatsoever."

Anton took out the paper that had been found in Frank Dekker's pocket and handed it to Lori. Felipe shifted on his feet just enough to call attention to his presence.

"This is your handwriting, Mr. Stone." Lori made clear it was a statement of fact.

The drumming of the rain was the only sound for several long seconds. Then, trapped in his own lies, Stone became confrontational again. "So what? I told him we would meet him when Mr. Cunningham arrived."

Cunningham took an audible breath, seemingly controlling his anger.

"That isn't what this says. It says you wanted to meet *both* people. Who was the other person, Mr. Stone?"

"The partner, Costa. When we met at their restaurant, it was clear to me that he wasn't sure about the sale and might hold up the deal while he looked into it. I wanted to make sure Costa was on board." He looked at Cunningham and nervously raised his voice. "It was a good investment—still is." He was pleading. "Think of it, Matt. A thousand-room resort with its own helipad."

Lori was stunned and trying hard not to show it. Matias Costa would never have agreed to such a development. From the start, he had been an ardent supporter of Anton's plan to conserve the land for future generations.

Anton's voice was loud enough to make everyone jump. "Not Costa!"

Lori reiterated what he said, "We are certain that Mr. Costa would not sign such a contract," and as she spoke, a piece of the puzzle fell into place. "He wasn't going to be told that was the plan, was he?" She watched Stone's eyes and continued, "He was going to be told that the land would be sold to people who care for it as he does." A dry swallow and a couple of rapid blinks told her she was on the right track. "That's what the call you made ...," Lori couldn't help looking at Eleanor Stone, "... you were *told* to make on the night of the 3rd was about." She looked at both the Stones. "You told Frank Dekker exactly what to say to Matias Costa, and he assured you the deception would work."

Anton had followed what she said and was now towering over Stone. Even Felipe had taken a few steps into the room, his face hard.

Cunningham's voice was cold when he said, "How were you going to arrange it, Harold? Pages replaced after he signed? A doctored contract?"

With those words, the reason for the second meeting became clear to Lori. "That's why you really wanted to meet on April 4th, isn't it? Matias Costa had to be there to sign a contract, but it would be a new contract, an altered contract."

Nearby, Eleanor Stone was fidgeting, while her sister kept her lowered eyes on the table.

"What did you give Dekker?" Cunningham asked.

"Look, nothing was signed. I did nothing illegal," Stone defended himself, "and the government plan was doomed to fail, anyway."

Out of the corner of her eye, Lori saw Anton flinch; he had understood.

Stone began to feel the upper hand. "It's true, you know. They couldn't have made money. But Costa just didn't get it. He wouldn't even consider a deal that would have set him up for life." His notion of right and wrong, success and failure, was so limited, the confession that followed sounded like a boast. "I was going to give Dekker a bigger cut of the profits, and he was going to convince Costa I had made another offer, one that would preserve his precious land even better that the government plan." He looked at Cunningham. "Our company would have made millions."

"*Our* company? You were never in this for *our* company, Harold. I know you. You're only in anything for your own good."

Lori thought of Hanson when she played her final card. "How much of that money was to have been *untraceable*, Mr. Stone?" His shock was written on his face.

Cunningham's threat was clear when he said, "I'll be comparing the profit projections that were generated with the ones that were delivered to me. That will show if—*how*—you intended to benefit personally. And I'll wager a close look at the books will show even more."

Stone's response was unexpected: there was a glimmer of triumph in his eyes. "Let's be careful about what we say and do, Matt. You don't want to risk everything you've worked for, and you certainly don't want to upset Carolyn, do you?"

Cunningham looked at his wife. Across the room, she sat with her elbows on the table, rocking her head in her hands. "That isn't going to work, Harold, not anymore. Carolyn and I have spoken. She knows that one way or another, all this is all going to end."

"You don't want to do this," Stone warned, but it was an effort to keep his voice steady.

Cunningham pointedly ignored his brother-in-law. He looked at Lori when he explained, "Carolyn is addicted to painkillers and has been for several years."

It was Eleanor Stone who whimpered.

"Her own sister was the one to convince me, first that it was not a serious problem, and then that Carolyn could never survive the ordeal of getting treatment for her addiction. And I must own up to thinking I could handle the problem myself."

The word *handle* came back to Lori. "You were going to make sure Jack Hanson did not sell any more pills to your wife?"

Cunningham looked genuinely ashamed of himself. "She was doing so much better until we took *Wit's End* down to St. John's in January. After we returned, Hanson was always hanging around. I put two and two together, and I offered him a deal: I would say nothing about what he was doing, if he stopped selling pills to Carolyn."

"He agreed?"

"Not at first. He defied me to do anything, so I ...," he took a deep breath, "... I paid him off, and for a while Carolyn seemed to be improving."

"What happened the evening I came in on the ferry?"

"I've become familiar with the signs ...," he glanced at his wife, "... so I was keeping an eye on Carolyn. I saw her sneaking off the ship." He drew himself up for a confession. "My temper got the better of me. I followed her and, when I saw she was about to get more pills from Hanson, I attacked him. I never meant for Carolyn to get hurt."

The two sisters looked unhappy but in different ways. Eleanor had suffered a setback; Carolyn was utterly defeated.

"I'm sorry," Eleanor Stone reached out to her sister, but she was shaken off. "I only ever wanted the best for you." Her concern would not have fooled the most gullible of people.

Expressionless, Carolyn Cunningham waved her sister away. "No. No. No more. Enough."

"My wife and I have spoken. She knows she is going to get help—or it is the end of our marriage."

Stone's eyes narrowed. "You know this could be the end of *everything*, Matt."

Cunningham addressed Lori. He sounded like the man she had seen the day she first arrived on Santa Maria, confident and in command of his world. "Ms. Moore, I will tell you right now, in the presence of witnesses, and I will publicly admit this to my board: I have been responsible for buying illegal drugs for my wife over the years."

Stone looked at his wife and shook his head, acknowledging defeat. Her reaction was swift and angry. She got up, slapped the table with her magazine, and spat at him, "Don't give me any of that! Poor little man couldn't do what he said he would. Poor *little* man couldn't make it work, even with help."

Cunningham ignored her outburst. "Harold held what I did over my head, knowing that if it were made public, my career might be over." He walked over to his brother-in-law. "Harold, your association with my firm ends as of this minute. You have thirty minutes to leave my ship." He was about to say something to his sister-in-law but closed his mouth.

Stone tried to muster some defiance. "How am I expected to get back home?"

Lori spoke up, "When you are released, there is a ferry." She nodded to Felipe, who unsnapped the police department's only pair of handcuffs from his belt and walked over to Stone, a look of pure joy on his face.

Lori had fallen easily into the routine of family life; in fact, she felt more at home making the evening espresso with the old machine on the kitchen counter at Casa do Mar than she ever had making coffee with the stylish Nespresso in her Manhattan apartment. She poured cups for Anton and Catarina, and the Trinity Detectives settled around the table.

Catarina told her husband about the motive they had all forgotten to consider: love. "The Dekkers did not have a happy marriage," she said, first in English and then in Portuguese.

"Not like ours," Anton said, slipping a cookie into his mouth.

Lori knew that what Catarina had said could suggest anything from a relationship that lacked a deep romantic attachment to one that was abusive. "What do you mean?"

"A couple of the teachers at the football match said that he was always criticizing her in public, ridiculing her background and lack of sophistication."

"Would that be enough of a motive to kill him?"

Catarina glanced at Anton, but he was intent on sampling some of the dried fruits decorating the crust of a large loaf of bread on the table. "It wasn't just that," she said, slowly choosing her words as she spoke. "Paolo's teacher said that Isabella had a long cut under her eye when she dropped him off one morning, and when she asked the boy what had happened, he said his papa hurt her."

When Catarina translated for Anton, she got his full attention. He found it difficult to swallow the corner of bread he was chewing, and he felt a need to put an arm around his wife. She took that as he intended it: he would never allow anyone to hurt her in that way.

She told Lori the rest of what she had heard. "Some of the mothers had noticed small injuries like that over the years. They were suspicious, but Isabella always had an explanation for what had happened, one that was just barely believable."

"Why wouldn't she have left him?" Lori asked, knowing halfway through her question that such a solution might not have been as obvious or as easy for other women as it would have been for her.

"Where would she go? She has no family, and it is hard to find work on the island."

Anton had followed their conversation. "No," he said. He had another explanation. "Paolo." He knew his own wife would sacrifice anything for her children.

As the night darkened, they were all thinking the same thing. *Perhaps Frank's murder was more about Isabella than anything else.*

12

Anton knew who had killed Frank Dekker, and why. The resolution would bring him no pleasure, though. Good people were going to be hurt.

Of everything Anton had heard about Frank, one story had stood out. It was the one Estela had told about how Frank behaved around Paolo. According to her, he ignored the boy completely—except when Isabella was around. What reason could there be for a man like him to take pleasure in acting like a good father—but only in the presence of his wife? He had turned the question over and over in his mind, and he had come up with a possible explanation, one he confirmed with a few phone calls, the first to Mr. Baretto, the Costa and Dekker lawyer in Ponta Delgada.

Anton left Catarina and Lori out of what had to be done, and he asked Felipe to wait at the police station. He returned to Water's Edge by himself. As was routine in the late morning, Isabella, Manuel, and Matias were in the kitchen, starting to prepare the day's meals.

"We all need to talk," said Anton. The seriousness of what he had to say was clear in his tone. Matias and Manuel looked at each other grimly. Isabella shivered and put on a sweater.

With everyone assembled around a table in the restaurant, he made a simple statement, "Isabella, Frank was not a good husband."

There was dignity in the way she lifted her head, looked him directly in the eyes, and said solemnly, "He was not." She offered no explanation.

"He beat you?"

She was about to answer when Manuel broke in, "Yes. My brother ...," he was reluctant to say the words. "My brother did what no man should ever do."

"Did you stay because of Paolo?" Anton asked Isabella.

She clearly did not want to answer that question. She looked helplessly, first at Manuel and then at Matias.

Matias spoke first, "Isabella is a good mother." It was another evasion.

"You love the boy, yourself, don't you, Matias?" Anton hated to see his ally and friend involved in what he had to do.

"I love him as a son."

"And you love Paolo, Manuel?"

Manuel was haggard and spoke with effort. "I do."

"In fact, everyone seems to have loved Paolo ... everyone but his own father. Frank only seemed to show his son affection at certain times."

Isabella moaned. Stationed on either side of her, the two men reached out to comfort her.

Anton repeated what he had learned that morning, what everyone already knew. "Frank was named as the father of a young—a very young—girl's baby. Her family on São Miguel threatened to expose him to the police if he did not claim paternity on the birth certificate and support the child. Mr. Baretto handled the legalities, and that was supposed to have taken care of everything."

Tears were gathering in Isabella's eyes. The two men fixed their attention on her. Matias nodded sadly, but Manuel's affect remained flat.

Anton continued with what he had learned when he called the young mother's family. "When Paolo was just a few months old, the girl went to Portugal and left her son behind."

Matias added something Anton had not known, "Her family told Frank she had died in a traffic accident in Lisbon, and they didn't want the responsibility of taking care of a child anymore. They insisted he take the baby into his home."

Slumped low over the table, Isabella's childlike voice seemed far away, "We hadn't been able to have children, and one evening Frank said he had been offered the baby of a single woman who did not want to keep it."

Manuel's bitterness was rising with memories. "Over the years, my brother tormented her. Whenever she did not do exactly as he wanted—and sometimes for no reason at all—he told her Paolo would have to leave. It was one story after another. The mother had returned. Her family wanted to raise the child. The adoption papers were faulty."

"When he told me he was the father, I wasn't even sure that was the truth," Isabella said limply.

"He threatened to take Paolo away to America," said Anton.

Isabella could barely be heard. "Yes."

"He was always threatening that," said Matias. "It gave him such pleasure."

Anger crept into Manuel's voice. "He wanted to hurt Isabella as much as he could. It was his way to do the evil he enjoyed doing."

Anton summed up the conclusion he had reached for the story Estela had told. "He played the role of a father when she was around—but only then—so she could see he claimed that role. It was to remind her that Paolo was his but not hers." He drew a deep breath, steadying himself for what would come next. "It was hard to see her pain."

"Yes," Manuel confirmed.

"Because you love her."

"I have always loved her."

Manuel's love for Isabella had been apparent to Anton from the first time he met them, as was that Manuel saw himself as her protector—from unpleasant questions, from distressing situations, and in all likelihood from his own brother. He laid a hand on Manuel's shoulder. "Why did you do it?" he asked gently.

"Francisco was a bad boy who grew to be an evil man."

"And this was your way to end the evil."

In the silence that followed, Anton heard his heart beating.

Isabella murmured, "Manuel, dear Manuel."

Anton turned to her. "The loss of your husband may not have upset you but when you realized Manuel was involved, everything changed." Anton remembered how the woman who had seemed untroubled by her husband's death was so different a few days later. Pale and weak, she had become uneasy talking to him and slow to agree that it was important to find the person responsible for her husband's death. She had even tried to mislead him with suggestions that a stranger might have killed Frank for money. "How did you figure it out?" he asked her.

Isabella was trembling. She shook her head, letting Anton know she would say nothing.

It didn't matter. He had a good idea. "You must have seen him follow Frank down to the beach that night, and after you had the time to think it through, you realized what had happened."

She said nothing to Anton. Instead she looked at Manuel tenderly.

One large tear snaked down Manuel's cheek.

Anton felt close to tears, himself. "Don't you owe it to Isabella to tell her what happened?"

"Leave her alone." He was stricken—not with remorse over what he had done, not with sorrow for himself, but with anguish for her suffering. "I—I didn't mean to do it. I was clearing glasses from the back patio, and I saw him go down to the beach. I went to tell him that I understood, that it was best for him to sell the land and go to America, because it was what he had always wanted. But the triumph in his eyes told me he had something wicked in mind."

Isabella sobbed softly and wrapped her arms around him. "Hush, dear Manuel."

He looked at her. "I knew he intended to hurt you."

"The hurt was only one part of my life, my dear protector. I still had Paolo. I still had you and Matias and Water's Edge. And Frank was going to America; I would have been left—," she broke off, a terrible realization dawning on her. "No," she said in horror. She pulled away from him, wide-eyed. "No. What did he say to you that night? What did he say, Manuel?"

Anton could see that Isabella already knew the answer. "Paolo," he said.

"This time he had plans," explained Manuel.

Isabella looked at Anton, her eyes remote and her voice drained of energy. "Frank always told me that he would take Paolo from me, that he could since Paolo was his son naturally, but not mine."

"What did he say to you that night?" Anton asked Manuel.

"After all the years, after all the beatings and all the threats, he was going to make good on his promise. He was taking Paolo with him to America. He already had passports for himself and his son."

It was finding out about the passports that had confirmed Anton's suspicions.

Manuel went on, his eyes unfocused as he remembered. "When I asked him why, he said Isabella would still have to do exactly as he wanted, even if he wasn't here. He said he had given her the life she had, so her life belonged to him."

Isabella took Manuel's hand and pulled it to her wet cheek.

He looked at her. "I didn't want ... I didn't want him to hurt you anymore. I don't even know what I was thinking. I was angry. I picked up the rock, and I hit him. Then I saw what I had done."

Isabella kissed the palm of his hand, and they both wept.

"This was found on Farewell Beach the morning after Frank died." Anton reached into his jacket pocket and took out the crucifix. "It's yours, isn't it, Manuel?"

"It was," he said with profound sorrow.

"When I first saw it, it was chipped here at the top, from when you put it down on the rock. The chip was still there the next morning, so you must have left it after high tide the night before."

"I did."

Earlier that morning, Anton had thought through his last visit to Water's Edge, and he had pinpointed the moment when Matias had started stumbling over his words and evading questions. It had been when Anton said he had seen the other crucifix; and almost certainly that would have been in connection with Frank's murder. "Matias, you must have known Frank never wore the crucifix. If he had, it wouldn't have mattered that I had seen it. You were protecting someone. You figured out Manuel must have killed Frank, didn't you?"

Matias felt deep pain. He knew his reactions had helped lead Anton to Manuel.

Anton held the crucifix out to Manuel. "It's yours," he said.

Manuel looked down at the crucifix with shame. "I took it off when I saw what I had done. I was no more entitled to wear it than he had been." He turned to Isabella. "I left it where we went to watch the night sky when we were young. Remember? Remember where we carved our initials into the rock? Manuel loves Isabella."

Anton's mind recaptured the image he had seen.

M V I

The scratches seemed to show three letters: M, V, and I, but there was no V. The top of a heart had worn away, just as the tops of the letters had. It was a testimony to the love they had once shared.

Anton offered Manuel the crucifix again, but he looked away. Isabella reached out and in one graceful move wrapped it in her scarf and placed it gently in his pocket. "This is yours, dear Manuel. Let it remind you that Jesus knows you are human just as He was. You did a terrible thing ... but you did it for love, and He forgives you."

Matias stood, tears running down his cheeks, came up behind Manuel and Isabella, and embraced both of them.

Anton waited for three friends who had shared their lives to say goodbye.

Manuel looked at Anton and said, "It is time." He didn't follow Anton to the door, though; he walked behind the bar and reached to the very back of a shelf, where he had hidden the picture of Frank and Isabella at their wedding. "Every time I passed this, I thought about how our lives would have been different if I were the one and not my brother." He removed the picture from its frame and tore it in half, saving the part that showed the face of the woman he had loved for thirty years.

He hugged Matias one last time, kissed Isabella on the forehead, and nodded to Anton.

Anton put an arm on Manuel's shoulder and led him away.

Wit's End was still being held at the marina. Anton went to personally let the Captain know his vessel and her remaining passengers were free to leave, and as usual the Minister's personal interpreter accompanied him.

It was early afternoon, so the marina was deserted, with windows shuttered and all boats tied down. *Wit's End*, large, white, and heavy, seemed to anchor one end of the dock. Anton would be glad to see it gone. It was out of place. He knew that some people, perhaps most people, wanted what they had on land with them on the water, changing only the view through the windows. That wasn't for him. Anton delighted in the differences between being on land and being at sea. In a boat he liked to sit close to the surface, rising and falling with the swells, feeling fresh winds and salt mist on his skin, close enough to see fish through the water, close enough to look dolphins in the eye.

They headed for the pilothouse but it made only as far as the stairs to the forward deck. Captain Sullivan's daughter sat on a step, texting. "They're up there," she said without taking her eyes off the screen.

Lori and Anton squeezed past her and walked out onto the polished deck. Carolyn Cunningham lounged in the shadow of an umbrella with Eleanor Stone beside her. Neither even looked up from their magazines.

Matthew Cunningham was at a nearby table, looking out to sea. When he saw them, he stood and extended his hand to Anton. "Please sit," he said, pulling out a chair for Lori.

"The Minister wants to let you know that Mr. Stone has been released to the American Consulate. He will not be allowed to return to the Azores," she said. "*Wit's End* is free to go, and Minister Cardosa apologizes for any inconvenience."

"I am the one who should apologize."

Lori drew her eyebrows together to question him.

"I was responsible for Harold while he worked for my company."

Lori said nothing, fully expecting him to stop short of owning up to how he had dealt with his wife's addiction.

He lowered his voice. "Carolyn needed help. I thought ...," he checked himself to verify what he was about to say. "I was wrong—,"

He broke off when a young woman carrying a tray appeared beside them. "Shall I set this up on the table, sir?"

Cunningham rose. "Please join us, Minister, Ms. Moore."

Anton was about to say that they were leaving but when he saw what was on the tray, his mouth started watering.

Cunningham finished business first. He directed his attention to Anton. "I wish you all the luck, but conservancy is not a direction my company wants to take, even if offered a portion of the land to develop."

Lori kept it to herself that Anton was not interested in developing any portion of the land. *It couldn't hurt to have him think he has disappointed us.* "The Minister does understand. In fact, he is welcoming representatives of the Gillis Foundation on Monday. They are considering sponsoring the conservancy of the entire parcel."

Anton had not understood what Lori said. He made an attempt to mimic the way Lori had pronounced *Gillis*. "Gillis no good. No airplane. Little time."

Lori explained, "The representatives are arriving in Ponta Delgada on Sunday, when there are no flights from São Miguel to Santa Maria, so they will have less time than is ideal to talk with us."

They spent an amiable thirty minutes sampling the refreshments and chatting. The self-possessed Cunningham unemotionally set out the advantages of living in big cities and—with limited English and a lot of enthusiastic gesturing—Anton defended the advantages of living in small communities; yet, despite having very different viewpoints and temperaments, the two men got along quite well. And they did find themselves in complete agreement on one thing: the magnificence of the ocean.

Anton's face lit up when he said, "Come to Casa do Mar five days, six days. Beautiful oceano Atlântico. Anton will be ... amigo." He laid a hand on Cunningham's back to let him know he was offering his friendship.

"Thank you. I will return to the Azores next year, and I will visit you then. If we are to be friends, however, you should call me Matthew." He offered Anton his hand, and they shook warmly.

Cunningham thought a moment. "I am truly grateful for how you dealt with Hanson, and kept Carolyn and me out of it." He glanced at his wife, who appeared to have dozed off under her umbrella. "I would like to bring your visitors here overnight tomorrow and return them to São Miguel late on Sunday—that is if they wouldn't mind a couple of nights on the high seas," he added lightheartedly. "I promise to show them a good time, and to deliver them well-rested and ...," he looked at Lori, "... ready to listen with open minds."

His look said even more than his words. She knew he might hint at his own interest, perhaps even say he was deferring to the Gillis Foundation in the interest of preserving an island as special as Santa Maria. She couldn't imagine a more auspicious start to the visit.

13

It was the twentieth anniversary of Anton's and Catarina's wedding. The day had its own traditions, understood and honored by everyone in the family. Liliana and Toni made passable pancakes for breakfast, while their parents looked through a box of cards, pictures, plane tickets, diplomas, baby bracelets, and other mementos collected during their life together. They read aloud from old letters, and they laughed at their teenage words.

They brought pictures of their parents to the table and shared stories about them with the children. Petrus Vanderhye, tall, fair, and ramrod straight, had lived into his eighties, never reconciling with his daughter's choice of a husband. Lisolotte Vanderhye's most recent picture, sent two years earlier when she had last responded to her daughter's frequent notes, showed her looking frail in age, her hair dull and sparse, and her facial skin drooping. The emotions their faces had evoked when Catarina was a child came back to her unexpectedly, making her feel proud or discouraged, lifted up or beaten down, as she showed the pictures.

By contrast, Anton's parents, Maria and Carlos, remained as they were when he was a teen. At that time, he had thought of them as old, but he no longer did. He was approaching the age they had been when they died. He could still hear their voices, his mother promising to show the woman he married how to make his favorite foods, his father talking about how much his world had changed since he was a boy.

"When did you know you were in love?" Lori asked.

Anton had understood the question. He pointed to himself and said, "Anton love Catarina when fifteen years." Then he pointed to Catarina and said, "Sixteen years. Young. Yes. Very young. But love very much."

He pecked Catarina's cheek, and she held a hand to his.

Liliana and Toni were giggling. Both knew the story well and, overlapping with one another, they told it while Anton groaned and Catarina looked on indulgently.

"Papa was a bad boy." At that remark, Toni got a gentle swat to the back of the head from his father.

Liliana tsk-tsk'ed and wagged her finger at Anton. "He did not do his homework."

Anton hung his head in mock shame.

Toni giggled freely in the way children do. "Papa liked only to play football." He glanced at his father and added with pride, "He is excellent playing football."

"Mama was the best student on all of Santa Maria. She was going to university. Papa—,"

"Papa was not going to university," Toni picked up the story.

"He would be without Mama," Liliana theatrically dabbed pretend tears from her eyes.

Catarina stepped in. "Two years after we met, I told him I was going to university, and I would go with or without him."

Anton mimed crying. "Oh no, my Catarina will be lost to me. I say, 'Please not to go. Please. I love you.'"

"I knew he loved me, and I knew I loved him," Catarina said, "but I also realized life would be very hard for him if I had a degree, and he did not. I told him if he convinced me he would go to university, then I would change my plan to attend Oxford. I would go to university in Lisbon, instead, so we could be together."

"*Uma mentirosa!*" With a grin, Anton declared his wife a liar.

Toni tried to control his laughter as he shook his head. "Mama did not say the truth."

"I wasn't going to change my plans," explained Catarina. "I had already decided I would go to Lisbon."

"For to be near Anton," her husband said with love.

"Mama made Papa work," said Toni with delight.

"Oh, such work." Anton dramatically wrung his hands in anguish. "Four hours study every day. Every day!"

"Mama helped Papa," said Liliana.

Anton hung his large head and nodded slowly. "Then she goes to Lisbon. Poor Anton is alone."

"But Papa became a good student." Liliana wrapped her thin arms around her father's neck with a proud smile on her face. "When Mama was at university in Lisbon, he still studied."

Anton added, "Every day. Yes. Every day."

Catarina was also proud. "Anton joined me a year later, a very well read man, and he got a degree with honors."

"When did you decide to marry?" asked Lori, pointing to her own left ring finger.

Anton laughed. "I say to me, 'Anton, this is perfect woman for to make you happy man—and more—good man.'"

Lori could see that was exactly what had happened. "When did you know you wanted to marry him, Catarina?"

She could tell Lori what had been said word for word. "He asked me, 'Are your parents kind to you?' When I told him they were not unkind, he said, 'That is not enough. I will make sure you always have kindness.' It was then that I knew I could count on him for the rest of our lives."

In the quiet that followed, everyone thought private thoughts.

Anton considered his great fortune in life, and he attributed all of it to Catarina. Without her, he would not have an education, and he would not have a purpose in life. Most of all, he would not have the family he adored. He looked at her and marveled that she had ever agreed to marry him.

Catarina, too, could hardly believe Anton had chosen to share his life with her. She thought about what he had brought her—security, happiness, connections to people and community and culture. He had given her the family she loved with all her heart.

If asked, Lori would have sincerely said that she enjoyed the stories of courtship and being included in a celebration of the love they all shared ... but a sad voice reminded her that the stories were not hers, and soon she would not be part of their lives. *I am only borrowing a place in this home, borrowing a place in this family.*

Just before the traditional anniversary dinner of roast chicken and celebrity custard with blackberry jam, Catarina finished wrapping her gift to Anton. He had always felt a special connection to people whose cultures were threatened or lost entirely—Jewish Kurds, Armenians, Native Americans, and most recently Syrians, and each year she found him a book on one of those cultures.

Anton's car swooped down the driveway. When he didn't appear in the kitchen, Lori went outside to look for him. He was bending over the retaining wall and peering into the bushes.

He looked up, saw Lori, and waved her away. "I will come," he yelled.

Soon after, his head appeared at the kitchen window. He put a finger to his lips to let Liliana and Lori know not to say anything. Then he mimed that he wanted Catarina to cover her eyes. He had a surprise.

Liliana giggled and took her mother's hand.

"What do you want, my little love?" Catarina asked.

"You must sit right here and not look."

Toni saw his father at the window. "Close your eyes, Mama!" He ran over to her and put his small hands lightly over her eyes.

"We are ready," Liliana called out in English.

Anton tiptoed into the room, a large bundle hidden under his jacket. "Open your eyes, my darling red-haired girl," he said.

Catarina opened her eyes, and watched as Anton unwrapped his gift to her.

Toni was the first to react with a murmured, "Ohhh."

Liliana said, "Mama, look!"

Catarina cried.

Anton held a sleeping puppy in his arms. "You are home," he said, as much to his wife as to the puppy, and his eyes glistened. He placed the warm ball of black fur in her lap and whispered, "No one will ever take your home from you."

Catarina became the little girl who had been denied a dog for so long. Cradling the puppy, she said softly, "My dog. My little dog. The best dog on the entire island. The best dog on all the islands."

14

Matthew Cunningham had lived up to his word. When Anton and Catarina saw their visitors disembark from *Wit's End*, they looked relaxed and happy to be on Santa Maria.

Miss Gillis was much younger than Anton had expected, probably in her mid-twenties. Tall and quite slim, her most notable feature was shoulder-length strawberry blond hair that stood out against a fashionable blue and white dress. Mr. Wright, on the other hand, was exactly as Anton had expected he would be, a mild-mannered older man, friendly enough, but serious and ready to get down to business.

While Mr. Wright greeted them with a courteous handshake and said, "I'm looking forward to getting started," Miss Gillis smiled brightly, removed her large sunglasses and said, "Hi. I'm Meghan. Are you the Cardosas?"

Before looking at the land the Gillis Foundation was being asked to conserve for the people of the Azores, Anton took the representatives on a tour of the island. Thanks to a stern warning from his wife, he was on his best behavior, driving as slowly as he ever had and keeping to the smoothest roads. Never had he regretted his poor English more. He knew only that Catarina sounded confident when she responded to the questions Mr. Wright peppered her with—although the *ohs* and *ahs* Meghan uttered every time a new landscape came into view did bring him guarded optimism.

For the most part, Catarina let the panoramic views speak for themselves. She answered Mr. Wright's many questions in words that faithfully expressed Anton's love for their land and his hope for the future of their culture, and she acknowledged Meghan's heartfelt admiration with great pleasure.

Anton pulled the car into an overlook with astounding views of the coastline and got out. In his limited English, he invited his guests to join him. He offered Meghan a pair of binoculars, carefully polished the night before, and pointed to several of the villages that ringed the island, giving the name of each. "Old," he said. "Very old. People come from very old people."

Catarina explained, "Most Marienses today have a history that started with the first people who arrived on the island and settled villages such as those."

Mr. Wright took many notes but only a single picture: the long crescent of fine white sand and clear, blue water known as *Praia Formosa*. Catarina proudly told him, "It is a Blue Flag beach, as you know an international award only given to the highest quality eco-friendly beaches."

"Well deserved," Mr. Wright commented, and Catarina winked at her husband.

Anton looked over his guest's shoulder and was very happy to see him writing down what his wife had said.

Meghan, on the other hand, took no notes but many pictures on her tour of the island. Catarina saw that as a reflection of how impressed she was by what she was seeing, but Anton was uneasy about what she was drawn to: terra cotta roofs green with mold, discolored limestone facades, rusting cannons, fountains mottled by algae, retaining walls crumbling from the effects of salt water and strong winds.

They stopped at an intersection, so Meghan could photograph the faded Moorish-style tiles on which the names of the two roads had been written for hundreds of years. It was there that Catarina made what would be the most memorable remark for their visitors, "Whether old tiles or old ways of living, the people of Santa Maria recognize their unique beauty and special value, and we are not eager to replace them."

After touring the land that had been safeguarded through generations of Costas and Dekkers, Anton took his guests to Water's Edge for dinner. Most islanders would have been shocked to find the restaurant filled to capacity three hours before it usually started serving. They would not have known that this was part of Anton's careful presentation. With help from Matias and Isabella, he had invited people who represented the heritage of the Azores—lace makers, boat builders, farmers, masons, potters, vintners—all of them descendants of the first settlers, and all of them still working in ways that had been passed down to them by their ancestors. Throughout the special meal, they stopped by and told their stories to the visitors from the Gillis Foundation. The last were Matias, who showed them around Water's Edge and told its history, and Paolo, who made a short speech that reflected how he, too, cherished his heritage.

It had been Lori's idea to stay out of the picture while the Gillis Foundation representatives were visiting. She had done her part. The rest belonged to Anton and Catarina.

She laid out the presentation booklets, and wrapped the parting gifts of seashell fossils found on the island, traditional honey cakes known as melindres, and fortified wines made on Santa Maria. Just before Miss Gillis and Mr. Wright were due to arrive at Casa do Mar, their last stop before returning to *Wit's End*, Lori left for a walk on Farewell Beach. As it did with Catarina, the little black puppy followed her closely—which was why she had been named *Sombra*, Shadow.

It was a lovely April afternoon. Casa do Mar lay peacefully under a soft blue sky, its two goats nibbling at wildflowers. The nearby creek, swollen into a cascading stream after the heavy rainfall, made pleasant soothing sounds, and a faint whispering could be heard from the forest whenever a light breeze stirred the leaves. Otherwise it was quiet.

Lori stopped at Casa do Bosque. Set in a grassy area that rose gently to the fence of the nearest neighbor's farm, it was encircled by the hydrangea bushes that were emblematic of the Azores. The little shed had been transformed. She stood back and admired Beto's handiwork. The exquisite precision of the way the stones were placed and the freshly painted shutters made it look as it must have when it was first built, two hundred years before. In front, a simple garden had been planted with roses, blooming in profusion and perfuming the air, and a small fig tree shaded the entrance. Two of the mothers from the school had come the day before and planted clumps of bright pink flowers in the window boxes.

Lori went inside. By the entry, eight identically framed photographs showed the renovation of Casa do Bosque and brought back pleasant memories. Thanks to enlarged windows, the cottage was light and airy, and thanks to Catarina's homey touches, it was welcoming. An arm chair was placed in a nook by the fireplace, and the table next to it held a vase of flowers and a few books.

Lori took a seat, and her thoughts began to wander. *My two weeks on Santa Maria are almost over.* An image of her New York apartment came to mind, and it seemed a drearier place than it had before she left. She felt a sadness filling her; but she had made her way through life by pushing such sadness aside, convincing herself that she was fortunate to have what she did, and carrying on with her life. *I will return, and I will start a new career. And I will be fine.* She tried to think through what she should do when she returned to the city but couldn't. She tried to think through what would satisfy her but couldn't come up with *what*—only *where. I'd be perfectly content to live right here.*

She reminded herself of the feelings she had had at Anton and Catarina's anniversary celebration. *I am only borrowing a place in this home, borrowing a place in this family.*

She got up and quickly walked to the door. On the way, she passed the watercolor of Casa do Bosque that Catarina had wanted to finish in private. She felt the pang of impending loss when she saw the tiny images of the family. Liliana cuddled with Sombra. Toni kicked his football. Anton and Catarina stood side by side watching them. And under the fig tree a woman sat, her long, blond hair blowing in the wind, her gray eyes looking out over the vast Atlantic Ocean.

Lori had known the most likely outcome of the visit from the Gillis Foundation before she ever set foot on Santa Maria, but she had been so carried away by the events of the past two weeks, she had not thought to forewarn Anton and Catarina.

Lori saw them approaching, deep in conversation, their figures close together against a dimming sky. Catarina took off the warm shawl that usually hung beside the kitchen door and wrapped it around her, and they clung to each other. *Minha amiga*, thought Lori, and she silently thanked both of them for sharing their family.

Catarina stepped back and cupped Lori's cheek in her hand. "We all did as much as we could," she said with a genuine smile. "Both Mr. Wright and Miss Gillis listened carefully, and they were favorably impressed, but the Foundation is seriously considering several other proposals." She took a breath. "A decision will not be reached for another year."

Anton laid a hand on Lori's shoulder. "Sorry," he said.

He said a few words to Catarina, and she translated. "Anton wants you to know that everything you did was perfect, more than he had ever expected." She lowered her voice and added, "On the way down to the beach, his biggest concern was how you would take the news."

Tears filled Lori's eyes.

"There is no need for sadness, Lori," Catarina said. "While we wait to hear from the Gillis Foundation, we will petition the court to approve the sale of the land, or at least its conservancy until Paolo is eighteen."

"More English one year," Anton said, and his cherub's face grinned.

Catarina laughed. "Now he wants to tell you that he will also learn more English while we wait."

"Yes," he said gravely.

Lori did not expect the good news that followed, and both Anton and Catarina gave her full credit for it. Meghan Gillis had been enchanted with Casa do Mar and with how a centuries-old shed had been converted to a charming guest house—so much so that she wanted to see what could be made of other parts of Casa do Mar. It was what Lori had hoped would happen.

Catarina's eyes were shining when she said, "She will lend us the money to restore another building but, since the loan will come from the Foundation's investment fund, it will have to be repaid with interest within three years." She looked up at her husband, his large figure silhouetted against the pink and purple clouds that hung at the horizon. "We have a lot of work ahead of us if we are to bring guests to Casa do Mar and make the first payment on time."

"Not a problem," he declared. "Anton has a plan!"

The first evening star appeared, and Lori made a wish.

Coming in 2016

Death at the Crater's Edge

It is a place that speaks of lifelessness: Capelinhos. Capelinhos, where the ocean boiled and the air filled with poisonous gas. Capelinhos, where the ground juddered with hundreds of earthquakes in a single week and peaceful villages were wiped from the face of the Earth. Now, the crosses of buried church steeples and the peaks of a few houses protruding through volcanic ash are the only signs that people once called this place home.

Anton thought the woman lying face up on the moonscape of Capelinhos looked very much at home, as though she had just levitated through her ash tomb and broken the surface to stare at the blue sky overhead in disbelief.

The Trinity Detectives, Anton, Catarina, and Lori are back, along with old friends and new visitors to the Azores. *Death at the Crater's Edge*, the next book in the Azores Heritage Mysteries series, is set on Faial.

My sincere thanks to—

—*My daughter, Amelia, who encouraged me to start writing and continues to encourage me with absolute faith.*

—*Kris Paulsen, editor extraordinaire, whose care and wisdom can be found throughout the book.*

—*Mia Boelman, whose careful reading and brutal honesty helped to make the book better.*

—*Rosemarie Capodicci, noted expert on the Azores, who started me on a voyage of discovery through my roots, and who continues to provide support.*

—*Kristina Fontes, an author in her own right, who helped with authenticity by advising me on the customs and language of Santa Maria.*

—*All those who share roots in the Azores and reached out to me in friendship after the publication of* Saudade.

Printed in Great Britain
by Amazon